The Infant Spirits

JANICE TREMAYNE

Edited by Kristin Campbell, C&D Editing—United States
https://cdediting.weebly.com/
Published by Millport Press
Printed and bound by Amazon.
ISBN: 978-0-6489615-8-1

DEDICATION

I dedicate this book to all my loyal super fans. You know who you are, and thanks for being part of my author life.

CONTENTS

ACKNOWLEDGMENTS

I want to acknowledge my fans for their kindness and support. Some have voluntarily offered their perspective as part of my launch team and invested their precious time in helping me achieve a quality product.

I want to thank my award-winning cover designer, Momir Borocki, for designing a stunning visual cover.

A book cannot reach its full potential without a great editor, and I'm grateful to Kristin Campbell for polishing up my work and making it read well.

Although I'm the author of this book, I'm not a singular entity. I recognize that it was the kindness of the people around me who motivated me to complete my passion for writing.

1 THE LADIES COTTAGE

New Norfolk, Tasmania 1878

"Get these bloody chains off me!" Abbey tugged rigorously, trying to free herself from being tied to the hospital bed. They were thick iron so strong that it was beyond her strength, but she kept on trying anyway, with a fierce intensity from within.

The bed shook vigorously with each jolt as nurses watched on, unperturbed by her efforts to free herself. They had seen it all before. Except, this time, it was different—she was pregnant and on the cusp of giving birth.

"Ya know she'll lose her baby if she keeps this up, poor soul. May the Lord have mercy on her," Nurse Delaney said. She was the most experienced psychiatric nurse at The Ladies Cottage. The younger ones took notice of her every word, and some doctors dared not cross her.

Nurse Louise gulped and nodded in acknowledgment, doing her best to maintain her composure under the circumstances. "Is she always like this? I mean, this agitated?" She was petite and a newly graduated nurse who questioned everything, and sometimes Delaney couldn't be bothered clarifying every point.

"Ah Louise, I've known Abbey for a while, and her family, too. I thought she was making a recovery at one point until …" Delaney stopped, realizing she was about to say too much.

"Until what, Miss Delaney?" Louise wanted to know more.

"Nothing. It's not important. Be a good nurse and help me hold her legs down before those chains rip into her ankles and cut her skin. We don't want a bloody mess on those white sheets, do we?"

"You're dirty rotten, Delaney, you witch." Abbey kicked as hard as she could, but Delaney felt capable of handling her outbursts. She was more robust than Abbey, whose frail body was no match for the hard taskmaster with the nickname *Haggus.*

"Just ignore her language, Louise. She'll calm down after the doctor gets here with the morphine. It will knock her out, I hope."

"You're a demon, Delaney. Fess up and stop hiding behind that nurse's uniform, as if you're the moral light of this cursed place!" Abbey lifted her head and spat toward the nurse, narrowly missing her face with the thick, yellowish mucus that stuck onto her white uniform.

Louise placed her hand over her mouth and nearly chucked. She was an inexperienced nurse, used to the private hospitals in Hobart for dignitaries and the rich. However, she'd had no option but to work at Willow Court Asylum, following her husband's posting to nearby military barracks.

Abbey continued her rage, holding on to the belly with both hands and pressing slightly in a futile attempt to stop the pain that was ripping through her body. She was eight months pregnant and was giving birth to a pre-mature, illegitimate child. No one knew who the father was, and nobody cared. That was the way it was back then, with a woman caught destitute in an asylum and locked away from the rest of civilization. They turned a blind eye to sexual assaults by staff that were commonplace amongst the patients.

"How do you do this every day, Miss?" Louise asked.

"Ha, I was once like you—all innocent and pompous—until reality set in. Oh yes, this isn't just any asylum; these patients are paid customers, set up by their families, hidden from view by the wealthy of this new land and godforsaken British outpost. A cursed penal colony, this is." Delaney continued pressing on Abbey's legs so she would avoid injury. "We're paid well to look after them, you know … whether we like it or not."

"I curse my family and those bastards for putting me in this wretched place," Abbey said. She was not worried about being outspoken. It made no difference to her life that was already ruined.

"And that Irish bastard O'Hara I always see you with, you bitch. He raped me in my room at night more than once, and you didn't do a thing about it. Miss Delaney, almighty nurse … ha-ha. Does your new girl know what you're really like? You're a demon you know, cursed by the devil himself."

"Best you put your hands over your ears, my dear," Delaney told her young protégé. "The demon has taken over her soul, and the poor child soon to be born."

Louise did exactly as she was told and placed her hands over her ears. It looked naïve from a distance, but she did whatever Delaney asked her to do.

Abbey continued kicking and clasping her hands as she helplessly tried to remove the chains. Delaney knew it was only a matter of time until her strength ran out. It was about persistence in these circumstances.

These intense bursts of anger and energy were all part of the fabric of Abbey's personality and why her family shunted her into this private asylum. Out of sight and out of mind, it kept the family's reputation untarnished.

Abbey was the victim of high society and their nefarious ways of thinking. And, although she was placed in the best mental asylum in the state that money could buy, she was denied the sort of existence worthy of her family's fortune.

"Where's that fucking doctor you promised!" Abbey was incensed that she had not been cared for properly by Dr. Jordan.

She was not a high priority for the brash psychiatrist. The only thing that kept her from being entirely neglected was her family would regularly check in each month. And nobody on the medical staff wanted to double-cross her influential sponsors.

Dr. Jordan came running in with his pediatrics colleague, Dr. Monserrat. Between them, they blew enough cigar smoke to fill the room with the secondary tobacco mist.

"Why's Abbey tied to the bed?" Dr. Jordan asked, looking directly at Delaney, knowing perfectly well it had been her decision to put the young woman in chains.

Delaney shuffled her hands nervously, realizing she had to explain herself. "Oh, Doctor, you know what she's like—behaving erratically again. It's for her own safety … and her unborn child."

"And your safety? Or perhaps it's something you like doing, Miss Delaney? You've been chaining up several patients recently. Part of a new game of yours?" Dr. Jordan didn't care about Delaney's influence, and he was prepared to stand up to her.

"You know she can be a difficult patient, sir, when she's in her moods." Delaney took the keys from her pocket and held them toward the doctor defiantly. "I suppose you want me to remove them, sir?"

He snatched the keys from Delaney in a show of contempt and walked toward Abbey. Then he placed his hands over her head, gently caressing her. "It's all right, Abbey. I've got Dr. George Monserrat here to look over your child. He's a pediatrician from the hospital; you can trust him."

Abbey seemed to react favorably to the doctor, whereas Delaney could not—a different style and approach used to care for mental patients.

He waved toward Dr. Monserrat and asked him to come over and assess her pregnancy. He was a mild-mannered man, a descendent of aristocracy, and well-regarded amongst his fraternity. And, like Dr. Jordan, a younger man with different points of view toward the care of his patients

"May I, Miss Abbey?" Dr. Monserrat placed his stethoscope on her belly as he listened to the unborn child's heartbeat. "I'm just going to feel the position of the child now."

Abbey remained still as tears rolled down her cheeks, a release of tension, no doubt from being tied up by Delaney and her cruel methods.

Dr. Monserrat rubbed her forehead and patted her curly, mousy brown hair from her eyes. "It's okay, Miss Abbey. Everything will be fine."

He continued to inspect the position by pressing her belly. "Oops, that's a nice kick. Did you feel that, Miss Abbey?"

She smiled, her glowing white teeth evidence of her wealthy background. "I felt it all right, Doctor. It's not the first time my child has kicked like that."

"Oh, that's a good sign, then. An active, kicking child, he is." The doctor covered her belly with a white sheet then placed his stethoscope back into his side pocket. "You're close to giving birth, miss. It could be any time now."

Dr. Monserrat looked toward Delaney and said, "She's ready to go into labor. No chains to the bed. Take her to the maternity ward and care for her like you would for any mother ready to give birth. Contact me when her waters break and starts having contractions. No delay. Understood?"

Delaney nodded. "Yes, sir. Of course. We'll monitor her." She was not going to cross the line against a doctor with a hint of aristocracy in his blood.

Abbey raised herself with her back upright against the headboard. She rubbed her hands to relieve the red marks from the chains that she had furiously fought to get free from. She was in her late twenties and, despite her mental condition, was a beautiful woman. She had a face so attractive that any man in his right mind would seek her courtship. A perfectly shaped nose and hazel eyes that contoured into her soft, rounded face that was perfectly proportioned. Thick eyelashes that highlighted the intensity of her outward-looking complexion, complemented by perfect, white skin.

Dr. Monserrat waved Dr. Jordan to the side of the room, needing to discuss the condition of Abbey's pregnancy privately and away from Delaney.

"What's the issue, my man?" Dr. Jordan asked.

"There's something wrong with the position of the child."

"Tell me, Doctor."

"I've seen this before. Its heartbeat is elevated, meaning it's in stress." He paused to take a breath.

"And?"

"The umbilical cord is caught around the child's neck. They can both die in childbirth. The odds are abysmal." Dr. Monserrat turned his head side to side. "There's nothing I can do. She's in God's hands now."

Dr. Jordan looked at Dr. Monserrat with concern. It would have been impossible to avoid the glare of his bright blue eyes and contoured mustache rolled up on each side. "What's your best option? There must be something we can do."

"Hmm … High forceps delivery possibly, reposition the child … hope to God it responds and changes position without a fight so I can untangle the cord from around its neck. I need the head to be pointing in the right direction. But it's not been done successfully, and most mothers and children die from internal bleeding. In these cases, the child suffocates to death."

Both doctors stood quietly, looking at each other as they shuffled around nervously.

"Can you abort the child safely? You know that's the first thing the family will ask me," Dr. Jordan asked.

"I've heard about an abortion room next to the morgue, and I know it's a practice used in the past, but it's passed that time now. It's too dangerous a procedure."

Dr. Jordan sighed and clasped his hands. "I'm not like

my predecessor who had a policy of abortion in this place. It tormented the mothers and made them worse, some taking their lives. I stopped that practice when I started twelve months ago."

Dr. Monserrat gripped the other doctor's shoulder gently as a sign of understanding. "You're a good Christian man, and I know you would only suggest abortion to save the mother's life."

"I better tell her family the circumstances, then," Dr. Jordan reluctantly announced.

"What about Abbey? Are you going to tell her?"

Dr. Jordan paused and looked out into the passageway. If he was a machine, you would hear parts moving in sync in his head; such was his concentration. "How do you tell a mother that she could die during the birth of her child, and especially a patient deprived of the capacity to think clearly?"

"You mean, insane?" Dr. Monserrat turned to him to get his attention. "You can tell me straight, you know."

"Yes, insane and unable to cope with such news. Who knows what Abbey will do?"

He placed his arm over the shoulders of Dr. Monserrat and said, "Let's discuss this more over a cup of tea, my good man."

As both doctors made their way to the dining room, Dr.

Jordan turned around to Delaney and said, "I've heard things about the Irish maintenance man. I've forgotten his name. We need to talk about him tomorrow, Miss Delaney. Come to my office at nine a.m. sharp, and we can discuss it. Apparently, you know him very well."

"Oh yes sir, Mr. O'Hara. A good man he is, and he's been with us for a long time. We all know him very well. And he's well-liked by all of us, you know."

Dr. Jordan nodded, preferring to leave the conversation for later than form an early opinion. He wasn't a man who could be fooled so easily. In the last twelve months, a spate of pregnancies had piqued his interest; all paid patients of The Ladies Cottage wing of the asylum. The women were all from wealthy families who had paid to have them cared for. Yet, the hospital could not provide a reason for the unexplained pregnancies. The women rarely received visitors, besides family members, and the only men allowed in that section were doctors and the Irishman who worked as a maintenance man.

One woman, who had given birth only a month ago, had her child removed, fearing she was going mad. It was for her own safety and that of the child. The family had eventually agreed to take the child into their care. She was a woman who had a psychiatric condition that today would be described as bipolar. Still, she had never exhibited suicidal tendencies until the birth of the child. It had become an all too frequent scenario—women giving birth then becoming suicidal to the point they were a danger to their child.

Dr. Jordan called over the canteen assistant to ask for tea and biscuits. He ordered his favorite imported tea blend from Sri Lanka that was most popular amongst the staff.

"Have you noticed the nurses' carrying objects to ward off demons? A holy cross around their necks and gemstones with eyes to repulse demonic spirits," he said. Although a Christian man who regularly attended the local Catholic mass services every Sunday, he could see the staff's change in mood over the last six months.

"A deliberate concealment of objects linked to superstition, as an act to ward off evil," Dr. Monserrat responded with a likewise observation.

"Hmm … But there's more to it than just warding off demons."

"Tell me Doctor; what do you think is the cause?"

Dr. Jordan thanked the tea lady for his cup of tea and biscuits then took a sip before responding. "It's not just the staff; the patients are superstitious, too."

"Tell me more." Dr. Monserrat also sipped his tea, showing a sign of satisfaction in the blend. "Ah, very nice."

"For the patients, it's not just superstition. We have

found objects hidden in their rooms—under beds, blankets, and personal belongings. It's an act of power and control."

Dr. Monserrat creased his forehead and lifted his eyebrows in sequence. "I don't understand."

"By having these secret activities and space where they conceal things, it allows patients to control this part of their life, in a small way," he said.

"Yes, well that all makes sense. They're always under supervision, day and night."

"They live in the confines of this building, where they have no control over their lives; everything scheduled in terms of what they can do with their time," Dr. Jordan conferred.

Dr. Monserrat took another sip of his tea while dipping in a shortbread biscuit, still listening attentively. He admired Dr. Jordan and looked up to him as a mentor.

"This way, they can be in control of something and hide these objects that have significance. Even though, to other people, they might have looked like trash."

"Hmm ... If I was to rationalize this behavior, I would say they are creating a time capsule of important things. Hide them away where no one could stop them. They're an only sense of control," Dr. Monserrat said.

Dr. Jordan nodded. "Well-observed, Doctor. That's

exactly what I thought."

"But, how do you explain the staff's attitude in carrying objects to ward off demons?"

Dr. Jordan sighed and looked straight into the other doctor's eyes. "That's something we need to find out—what's driving this behavior amongst my staff."

"You mentioned the Irishman before to Nurse Delaney; what's your suspicion about him?" Dr. Jordan was straight to the point.

"This asylum takes in patients from all backgrounds across the state, and we separate them into different wards. This ward here, the paid ward, is where the pregnancies began twelve months ago."

"And there's only one man who works in these wards?" Dr. Monserrat asked. It was a leading question.

"Well, besides the doctors, yes. He works late when the staff are gone. He claims it's emergency repairs—plumbing mainly. He's always got an alibi."

"And backed up by the head nurse?"

"Oh, Delaney. She's another story, my good Doctor. Just watch your step with her." Dr. Jordan winked then tilted his head.

Dr. Monserrat nodded in acknowledgment. "Well, thank you for the tea and shortbreads. It was delightful."

"Oh, we're not done yet. I want to show you something

before you take off."

"What do you have in mind, Doctor?"

"I want to show you the abortion room you mentioned earlier. Nobody talks about it. Just the slight mention or a slip of the tongue and staff turn red in fear. They do everything to avoid a conversation on the topic."

"An odd practice. I thought abortions were illegal unless authorized, Doctor?"

Dr. Jordan finished his tea then stood up. "Yes, they are illegal, and so are many other things *I've* discovered in this place." He pointed to the hallway that led to the abortion room. "This way, my good sir. Follow me."

2 THE ABORTION ROOM

Willow Court Asylum 1878

Willow Court is a magnificent, old stone building built as a military hospital in 1830, by Major Roger Kelsall in Tasmania, Australia. Governor Arthur originally conceived Willow Court as a location where invalid convicts could be housed. It's the oldest asylum on the island.

This is the hospital for the insane in New Norfolk, Tasmania, a peaceful township on the banks of the Derwent River, thirty-five kilometers away from the state's primary city, Hobart.

Records show that violent female and male patients, considered dangerous, were kept in separate wards at Willow Court. Patients were also separated by class and gender. Patients suffered a wide variety of psychiatric illness, described as depressive or hallucinating; many of which we view and treat differently today."

There was a room at the back of the asylum, a place where nobody wanted to go—the morgue. And next to it, an inconspicuous room that contained a chair and a small metal table used to place tools for performing operative procedures. But it was not just any chair—it was used for abortions. A mechanical type that adjusted to perform an operation that was illegal and considered immoral at the time. But that never stopped the eccentric doctor from experimenting with his ideas.

"So, this was Dr. Pendergrass's playground?" Dr. Monserrat asked.

"Yes. It feels so sterile and devoid of life. Many women died here during failed experiment and abortive procedures. They were treated like animals so that he could achieve his aims. He had the perfect environment—mental patients that nobody cared about. Who cared if one or two died a month in the process?"

Dr. Monserrat turned toward Dr. Jordan and shivered as his eyes flickered. "You said experiments?"

"Oh yes, women from the psychiatric ward for Colonials of Willow Court. The poor souls had nobody to care for them. They were considered dispensable in the name of science."

"And no one noticed them missing, either … their

families and loved ones?"

Dr. Jordan nodded. "We found evidence of cruelty through experimentation. He used new tools and devices; dangerous techniques that were so experimental they were banned from being applied to delivering babies. Dr. Pendergrass used these techniques for premature, disabled and, worst of all, the aborted fetuses."

"So, he was specific in his experiments?"

"Yes, he had a target group that he focused on—the complicated cases of delivery. His argument was that they would have died in childbirth anyway, due to complications."

Dr. Monserrat casually walked around the room that was no bigger than ten-by-twelve feet. "It smells of death. You can feel it and sense it in the air." A chill went down his spine, and the hairs on his arms stood upright.

Dr. Jordan nodded, acknowledging his emotional intelligence. "It was only by accident we found this room when a funeral director walked in here by mistake, thinking it was the morgue. He was new to this place and shocked to find a woman bleeding to death and her dead fetus on the floor. Blood everywhere, and a smell so putrid his stomach curled into knots."

"It would have been a gruesome sight for anyone." Dr. Monserrat stood firm, looking directly at the abortion chair, imagining what it would have been like. He lowered his head and sighed. "A living hell of debauchery."

Dr. Jordan picked up an obscure-looking tool, twelve inches long, with a hook used to rip apart the fetus, killing it instantly during removal. He pointed it toward Dr. Monserrat. "Here's an example of his handiwork—a tool that was banned by the Society of Surgeons years ago. He tried to get his techniques approved, including this piece of equipment, but failed, which only made him angrier."

"And he kept on using it despite their protests?"

"Well, not only that, but he modified it to make it more effective. He turned it into a killing utensil."

Dr. Monserrat closed his eyes and placed his hand on his head. "Well, then it was murder."

"Mmhmm … That's exactly why he ended up in jail and banned from ever practicing as a doctor again. Twenty years of hard labor for Dr. Pendergrass." He took a cigar and placed it in his mouth, moistening it with his lips. "But I've my suspicion that Delaney knew about this operation."

"Hmm … She does strike me as being someone with an evil streak in her. Did you see her face when we arrived to check on Abbey?"

"Oh yes, my good Doctor. Mark my words, she was enjoying every moment of having Abbey tied up so close to childbirth. That, I assure you."

Dr. Monserrat felt uncomfortable in the abortion room. "I think I've seen enough," he said.

"I've been in this room many times, and I always get the same feeling. I can't wait to leave after a few minutes. But something keeps drawing me back here—a calling or a spirit. So, I just keep looking around for anything of importance. But nothing. Just cold air and negative thoughts. Once, I saw a woman on the abortion chair. She was screaming as she looked deep into my eyes, begging for help, her arms stretched out, wanting to be saved. And these flashes only last for seconds then go away."

"Hallucinations?" Dr. Monserrat suggested.

"I wish it were that simple, my good Doctor. But I realized later that evil lurks in this room. A dungeon of misery, cursed by the screams of the dead women and their unborn children. It's about as close to hell you'll ever get."

Dr. Monserrat was silent as the doctor's forthright explanation sent a chill crawling up his spine that ended with a tingling sensation on the back of his neck. He shook uncontrollably as an instinctive reaction to the uncanny feeling that had gripped his body.

"Well, this isn't a good place to smoke, and I guess we better get going and check on Abbey." Dr. Jordan lit a match then inhaled deeply. He puffed on his cigar by creating an orange glow effect on the tip of the imported

Cuban brand.

"There's more to your story, isn't there?" Dr. Monserrat looked straight toward Dr. Jordan. He was an intuitive type who could read people's emotions, a natural skill he'd had since he was a child.

Dr. Jordan seemed preoccupied with his cigar and didn't respond right away. Then he shrugged and pointed toward the exit.

As they steadily walked toward the door, it slammed shut with a thumping *bang* that echoed through the small room, reverberating until the noise putted out.

Dr. Monserrat took a firm grip on the doorknob, moving it side to side. "It's jammed. It looks like we're locked in." He looked toward Dr. Jordan and brushed his eyes with his hands, a nervous reaction. "But you have the key, right?"

Dr. Jordan placed his hands in his white coat where he thought he had put the keys. "Oops. They're still in the lock outside, but it was unlocked. Here, let me try." He grabbed the doorknob forcibly then screamed in pain as he struggled to remove it. It was red-hot.

He clasped his hand in despair, finding his hand pink and blistered from the attempt.

Dr. Monserrat jumped to his aid, unsure what had taken place. "What on Earth was that? Good Lord!" He took him by the arm to the medical cabinet, where he pulled open the glass door then reached inside for a bandage and a bottle of soothing ointment. "Here, let me fix this."

Dr. Jordan continued to clasp his hand, shaking, his eyes scrunched, and his forehead creased in pain. "What the devil was that?" He pointed at the door. "Whatever you do, don't touch that doorknob." It was brimming red-hot, like an ironworker's furnace. They could not make any sense of it.

Despite the immense heat emanating from the doorknob, the room became colder. There was a chill in the air, and each exhale let off a visible sign of warm breath hitting cold air. It must have dropped ten degrees or less in an instant, as both men started to shiver from the elements.

"Give me your hand, Doctor," Dr. Monserrat instructed as he poured the ointment onto a white cloth then smothered the burn before wrapping it in a bandage.

Dr. Jordan shrieked in pain, as any contact on the pink blisters caused him to shrivel from discomfort.

"Why is it so damn cold in here?" Dr. Jordan asked as the cold air penetrated his fine cotton uniform.

"Hmm … If someone doesn't get us out of here soon, we'll freeze to death." Dr. Monserrat finished bandaging his hand. He then looked across the room to a small table containing leftover operating utensils used by the surgeon when performing abortions. One tool that was more than twelve inches in length with a flat edge caught his attention.

"If I bang on the door with that metal tool, someone should hear us outside."

Dr. Jordan nodded while holding onto the palm of his hand, still in pain. "If it's loud enough, a nurse will hear it down the hallway. Noise echoes in this place. I can make out the screams of patients down the hallway when I'm doing my daily visits."

As Dr. Monserrat walked toward the table with the operating utensils scattered in no order, a sharp object lifted from the table without assistance. Then it flew across the room, narrowly missing him, and fixed into the wall with a piercing sound, only inches from Dr. Monserrat's face. It was like the knife-throwing tricks used in a circus, except there was no magician in the room.

The table then started to rattle furiously, bouncing on its feet as it gyrated ninety degrees. Other sharp utensils flew off the table, unaided, harrowingly scraping past Dr. Monserrat's face, leaving a small scratch on his cheek this time.

"*Ouch!*" He placed his hand on his cheek then removed it to see a trickle of blood. Although it was concerning, the scratch was but a mere warning. Altogether, six sharp utensils were fixed to the wall surrounding Dr. Monserrat's outline. He didn't know what to make of it as he stood frozen, incoherent eyes glazed over.

"What's with the abortion chair?" Dr. Jordan asked, pointing at it with a delusional look. "There's a girl there … legs wide opened, and bleeding. She's in pain, holding onto her belly, grunting, and biting her lip. Her hands are tied to the chair, leather-bound. She's trying to break free. She's looking at me, goddammit! Her bright blue eyes are penetrating, but I can't hear her screams."

Dr. Monserrat walked toward him and slapped him across the face. "Snap out of it, man. I don't see any girl on the chair." He took hold of the other doctor's face with both hands and could see his eyes had become glassy, unresponsive, obsessed with the chair. Tears rolled down his eyes, though he looked emotionless.

"What is it, Doctor?"

"A dead fetus on the floor."

"What?"

"God help me, it's alive and kicking … covered in its own blood, and the umbilical cord is still attached. We need to save it. Save it!"

"I don't see anything, Doctor. You're suffering from hallucinations. The cold air, the burn, and the knives—it's all too much."

"Good Lord, evil lurks in this room. Can't you sense it, man?" Dr. Jordan felt the presence of an evil spirit. It was the transient soul of a mother and child who had tragically died in this theatre, the victims of experiments. It was a manifestation, angered and seeking retribution.

Dr. Monserrat glanced toward the wall next to them to find the six knives spaced out geometrically to form five letters, as thick, red blood trickled down at each entry point.

A message of some sort? he thought.

As the blood trickled down the wall, it curdled into a formation—into words—a message.

TULIP.

"What on Earth does that mean?"

Abbey was resting in the maternity room, holding her belly as her contractions became painful. In the early stages of giving birth, she was happy to be away from Delaney and her cruel ways. But she also understood it was only temporary, at least while the doctors were on site to keep an eye on her.

Delaney knew when to strike. A woman in her fifties, who never married or had children, you could understand why she had turned into a masochistic type. Working weird hours so she could turn up in the middle of the night, claiming she was on the graveyard shift.

But that was not true.

A woman who had no life outside her work, the asylum was all she had to keep herself together. But there was something sinister about her, and bouts of impromptu and uncontrolled urges that plagued her mind led to her deviant manifestations.

Delaney liked the same sex, and the asylum was a perfect playground, a window shopping bonus for her to look for her next lover. And because nobody found this plump, aging woman stacked with makeup, attractive, she would end up getting what she wanted by stealth. Unless, like Abbey, those who put up a good fight and stood up to her, which then led to retribution. Delaney preferred strong women like Abbey, and the challenge gave her satisfaction

All the women in the ward knew her tendencies and that the vulnerable ones were the pretty, younger women. Delaney preferred the ward where the youngest were separated from the senile patients.

But most deviants like Delaney, couldn't manage their terrifying tendencies alone. They needed support, and so she had found one in the sex-crazed Irishman, Marcus O'Hara, the maintenance guy. He also had a fetish for younger women. So what if he raped one girl a fortnight, or more frequently, when he felt the urge? They were mental patients, and their families barely cared about what happened within the asylum.

The dirty duo, as they had become known, did what they wanted without interference from the other staff. The longer-surviving nurses and assistants knew what was going on. Still, they were more concerned about their better-paid jobs and livelihoods. The gatekeeper who worked the night shift was lazy and slept through the night. He didn't care too much for what was going on around him, either. And the doctors who managed the asylum lived off-site in fancy homes, attending dinners with the town's social elite.

Delaney had it all worked out with the gatekeeper—a plate of hot scones and jam was all it took to pass through the gate. As for the sex-crazed Irishman, a small pint of whisky and an excuse to fix a broken water pipe was enough to get him across the line.

The families of these patients paid exorbitant fees to keep them out of sight from society. That was the deal to maintain their reputation as a line of respectable families at all costs. To keep the social elite of Tasmania good with their reputation for providing offspring to continue their line in society. The perfect family with no flaws to talk about and held in high regard.

As Abbey turned on her side to relieve the pain from her

mild contraction, she felt a presence in the room. A feeling in the air awoke her senses to something peculiar. It was a gentle vibration or a whisk of cold air, like someone breathing on you. A change in lighting as though a shadow cast over your body.

Abbey felt a tingling sensation in her toes, like being tickled with a feather. It was followed by something pressing gently on her legs—an evil touch and cold bone sensation. At first, she thought it might have been Dr. Monserrat coming back to check on her, but the ambiance in the room had changed unexpectedly as the glimpse of a dark shadow glided across the sterile white walls. It maneuvered quickly, and unless your eyes were focused on the right place at the right time, you would have missed it.

Abbey blinked more than once and gently shook her head, thinking it was the pain starting to affect her mind. Therefore, she thought nothing of it at first.

"*You'll die* ..." It was the voice of a cigar-smoking gentleman with a glass of brandy in the other hand; an educated tone.

Abbey looked around the room as she struggled to roll over to the other side of the bed, clasping her belly with both hands as she grunted to ease the pain. Turning from one side of the bed to the other was not easy, and she needed the aid of low-hanging leather ropes with a strap at the end. But there was only the empty expanse of a plain room; derelict of any facilities and typical of asylum at the time. Some dogs lived in more luxurious surroundings than mental patients. The fact that she had been placed in her own maternity room was a privilege, thanks only to the request of Dr. Jordan.

"And your son will die with you ... " This time, the voice was pronounced, as though feet away from her. It penetrated her ears and carved a way through to her mind.

"Who are you? Show your face." Abbey tried hard to raise herself along the metallic headboard to get a better view. "And, how do you know it's a boy?" Abbey might have been suffering from mental illness, but that didn't mean she wasn't sharp. "It's you, O'Hara, isn't it? You slimy bastard. Pretending to be on call, fixing something again?" Abbey took a walking stick next to her bed and raised it in the air. "Come within a foot of me, and I will split your head in two, you deviant bastard."

Although the voice had sounded like O'Hara's, it wasn't. He had a strong Irish accent, and this voice was that of an English gentleman. Abbey thought someone was trying to confuse her.

"Oh, it's not O'Hara, that filthy animal, my dear. And I don't blame you if you feel the urge to clobber him and split his head open. Imagine watching pieces of his brain splash onto the walls. Now that's a sight you've been waiting for."

"Who are you, if it's not O'Hara? What do you want?" Abbey struggled to lift herself upright on the bed that rattled and squeaked with the tiniest of movements. "Show yourself. What are you? A monster? A demon that needs to hide its disproportionate face?"

"Now, now, my dear, I'm only here to help." The voice rebounded off the walls, as though the poltergeist was pacing around the room. "I suppose the good old doctors didn't tell you?"

"Tell me what?" Abbey was incensed and raised her voice.

"Of course they didn't, just in case you panicked and couldn't control yourself." The voice paused for a short while. "They didn't explain to you that your boy is in a dangerous position, unable to turn in the right direction; its head pointed sideways, the umbilical cord caught around his neck. They want to perform a high-risk forceps delivery that no one has ever survived. Usually ends in death my dear, for mother and child."

"How did you come by this information? How do you know it's a boy?" Abbey's voice was becoming choppy and cracks appeared in her tone.

"Hmm … Let me come clean, my dear. I'm not from

this world."

"You're a spirit?"

"Nuh-uh, spirits float around all day, watching people going about their lives, confused and not even aware they are dead. Like a bad dream that never finishes, it just goes on and on …"

Abbey creased her forehead with a sharp look in her eyes. "If you're not a spirit, then why are you hiding? Or maybe it's a curse coming to haunt me … You're the devil's work, aren't you?

"Oh yes, the devil. I like that. It's better than being called an angel. How boring it would be, floating around all day, trying to appease their master by doing good deeds."

"You're a demon?"

"Nah, a poltergeist, ma'am. I sit between the spirit world and demon because it suits me. I'm a little closer to the physical world, so I can influence it. Sometimes, I can even touch it for a short while. Demons can't do that."

"And you can tell the future?"

"Ha-ha. That's easy once you get the hang of it. But it takes about a hundred years of experience as a poltergeist before you get it right. The first time I tried to tell the future, I made a mess of it. But that's okay because I frightened the living daylights out of her, anyway. I can still see her face of terror as though it was yesterday." The poltergeist took a twenty-second short break and didn't utter a word.

Abbey looked on quietly, trying to work out where the voice was coming from, but it was coming from everywhere, which confused her even more.

"You know it's a boy, and you say it won't survive the birth?" she asked.

"Oh, and neither will you. The doctors will mess it up so much that they will rip your organs and cause you to bleed to death from internal injuries. Ever tried to untangle an umbilical cord around the neck of an unborn child while in the wrong position? There's a lot of body parts to navigate around your uterus. It's a risky operation, my dear. Ninety-nine percent of women, and their children, die during this procedure." The poltergeist paused for a moment. "But in a way, I can't blame them for trying, because you're going to die anyway, if that makes any sense."

"I will die with my child?" Abbey's voice started to crack as a tear rolled down her face. She clutched her belly, immediately looking for signs of life, like the unborn child kicking or a heartbeat—anything to ensure her child was still with her.

The poltergeist sighed, as the conversation had become

a matter of routine. He was starting to get bored.

"But I can offer you some hope."

"How?"

"I will save you both from death's door if you can give me something in return." Although the poltergeist was not visible, the voice had a cunningness about it.

"What do you want? I mean, what can a dying woman and an unborn child give you of value?" Abbey always could pick holes in a conversation. It was the main reason Delaney never liked her—too intelligent and feisty for her liking. Asylum patients should be medicated, silenced and not heard. After all, they had been placed in the asylum by their families for a reason. They were insane and not capable of reasoning, let alone dismiss anyone's point of view in conversation.

"I will promise that both of you will survive the procedure. Your child's position will suddenly turn with his head facing down, in the right position, and the umbilical cord will no longer threaten to choke him. There will be no need for a procedure."

"A normal birth?" Abbey smiled then sighed, not wanting to express too much emotion.

"Yes, no need for a forceps procedure. Easy does it and ... *pop*, out comes a healthy newborn. Now, isn't that what we all want?"

Abbey nodded. "There's a *but*, isn't there?"

"Yes, just one small condition. That the soul of the child belongs to me."

"He'll never go to heaven?"

"Never. But I will look after him, like all the infant spirits. He'll have plenty of company like him."

"You've done this before."

"Oh ma'am, it's my pride and joy to create a spirit world of infants. It's a playground. You should see them having fun together. They don't think about their parents at all!"

"At what age will you take him?" Abbey's voice crackled with uncertainty.

"Ah, that's a good question. I get that from all the mothers. But, my dear, I'm doing a service to them and the child. Some mothers are incapable of looking after their child for whatever reason, and they usually *aren't* mentally stable."

"So, you think you're saving the child?"

"Oh, I never said that. That's what a priest would say, and I don't do good deeds. I just make deals. So, what do you say—die with your child or make a deal with me?"

Abbey was silent while she thought about the proposal.

"You want to give my child to the devil on the assumption he'll live in return? How can I believe you? You're a poltergeist." Abbey had a tear rolling down her face as she sobbed from the thought of making a painful decision.

"Hmm ... That's a good point to make. There's no hurry, and sometimes I need to let the situation evolve. I'll tell you what; you'll soon be in the delivery room, and the doctor will tell you about the procedure and why it's required. He'll leave it until the last minute, thinking you'll agree. All you need to do is call me out. Say the words, *take my child*, and it will be done. I will be there with you, watching over the situation with a glass of my favorite of brandy."

"Is this just a show for you? Entertainment?" Abbey was incensed.

The voice of the poltergeist faded away with his parting words. "Remember, just say the words, *take my child*, and it will be done."

Abbey was furious that the doctor had not explained her condition, placing her in a position where she had to agree to anything to save her child.

"Oh, and one thing, my dear. There's a one-page contract on the side table. I just need you to agree verbally—no need to sign it. And, don't worry; you're the only one who can see it." The poltergeist faded away again, and then the room returned to its previous ambiance.

Abbey was caught in a quandary, with a difficult

decision to make. Could she trust the dark spirit by forecasting the impending death of her child? Did the doctor's failure to provide her with the final prognosis mean putting her in a precarious situation? No matter which way she looked at it, she felt cheated and disrespected.

Time was running out for Abbey, as her contractions were becoming more frequent. The delivery of her child was but hours away. She had a decision to make to ensure mother and child survived the birth. It would be the most challenging decision of her life, and it was upon her.

3 THE CHILD TAKER

Abbey lay on her back in the delivery room, positioned for Dr. Monserrat to begin his perilous attempt at saving the unborn child and his mother. He was on his own, as Dr. Jordan had been called to another emergency in Ward C. Delaney was his assistant, though Dr. Monserrat wasn't comfortable with her, having formed a view about her cruel ways. But he had no other choice at this time.

He placed his hands on Abbey's abdomen and pressed firmly to determine the child's position. It had not moved, a bad sign. It was still gridlocked in a sideways position, its head pointing the wrong way. Dr. Monserrat sighed and took a deep breath as he removed his hands from her abdomen.

"It's really hurting, Doctor," Abbey said as she gasped for air then clenched her teeth.

"Abbey, I need to perform an internal inspection. It will be painful, but I need to feel the position of the child."

Dr. Monserrat looked to Delaney as sweat began pouring down the side of his face. "Give her the Twilight Sleep straight away."

Delaney nodded. "Yes, sir, straight away."

Twilight Sleep was an analgesic combination that relieved pain in those days. It caused women to forget most of their labor during birth. It had only become available recently in hospitals. Being a private ward, Dr. Monserrat had managed to secure the pain reliever months ago.

"This medicine will help relieve your pain, Abbey, while I inspect the child." He smiled at her and nodded to alleviate the anxiety levels that had built up throughout the day.

Abbey grinned, clasped her hands, and didn't say a word. Her expression was such she would accept anything to relieve the debilitating pain.

"Here it is Doctor, the Twilight Sleep." Delaney handed him the ampule containing the pain reliever and a needle.

"I'm just going to inject this into your arm, Abbey. You'll feel a sting at first, and then some pressure. It will be quick." The doctor injected the Twilight Sleep into her arm as Abbey squinted. "All done now. You should start feeling the effects soon."

As the Twilight Sleep started to take effect, Dr. Monserrat performed an internal inspection then shook his head. It wasn't good news. He knew he would have to perform the life-saving procedure with meager survival rates. The umbilical cord was still wrapped around the baby's neck, and he confirmed it was still in a sideways position.

"Can I have the high forceps, Delaney? The head is unengaged. I need to turn the child," he whispered impatiently.

Delaney handed the forceps to Dr. Monserrat with a concerned look.

As the doctor grasped the forceps into his right hand and was ready to insert the tool into the womb, the room's natural light faded. He found this unusual, considering it was in the middle of the day and clear skies outside. It was as though a dark shadow had passed in front of the windows, creating an eerie ambiance. The comfortable room temperature decreased to a chill too, as Delaney buttoned up her cotton, white-laced cardigan.

The doctor shivered as the hairs on his arms raised and goosebumps covered his skin. Trembling uncontrollably, he waited a while before he proceeded, knowing he needed a steady hand to move the child's head into the correct position.

"*I can save the young lady and her child if you agree with my proposal?*" It was a soft voice.

The doctor glanced toward Delaney. "Did you hear that?"

Delaney shook her head. "Hear what, sir?"

"*Oh, she can't hear me, Doctor. It's just you and me. And the poor girl is in so much pain she's almost delirious about anything going on around her.*"

"Delaney, please get me a glass of water from the kitchen." The doctor wanted her out of the room and to be alone with the poltergeist.

"*That's a smart move, Doctor, just you and me. And your nurse can't hear my voice, anyway.*" The poltergeist paused for a moment. "*Oh, Delaney, she has a filthy mind. Did you know that she likes the same sex? No wonder she loves her job. Think of the opportunities. It's a reservoir of potential suitors or, should I say, victims of her lust.*"

Dr. Monserrat didn't want to engage in conversation and was straight to the point. "Who are you, and why can't I see you?"

The room darkened another shade as an ominous shadow appeared in front of him. It was barely visible but enough to get an outline of a demonic figure. It was a devilish shape with horns and bat-like wings, standing on hooves at almost seven feet tall. It resembled a half-man and half-beast.

"Like I said, Doctor, I usually don't like making an appearance—I'm a private person. But let me put a proposal to you."

The doctor looked toward the shadow where the voice originated and continued to hold his silence.

"What do you say? The child will die, and you know it. You haven't told the young lady anything either, so she has no idea she's twenty minutes away from dying."

"And, what's your offer?" Dr. Monserrat clutched his coat nervously while trying to maintain self-control.

"I can save the child and mother. They can live a good life together ... but the soul of the child is mine, and I can take it any time after ten years of life ... at my discretion, of course."

"You want the soul of an unborn child with a guarantee you'll not take it away from the mother for ten years?"

"Hmm ... You are as sharp as they say, Doctor. That's the deal. Take it or leave it. And by the way, it's a boy."

Dr. Monserrat lowered his head and placed his fingers on his chin in pensive thought. The poltergeist was correct in his assessment—the chances of mother and child surviving the procedure was less than five percent. In Dr. Monserrat's opinion, this complication was considered a death sentence in most cases.

"Save the mother and child and take me instead. You can have my soul."

The demon scoffed at Dr. Monserrat's counterproposal. "*I'm flattered with such a request, but it's not you I want, my good Doctor. You don't have qualities that would be useful to me. It's the child I want. It's not a negotiation. Take it or leave it. I assure you the child and mother will die. You know that.*" The demonic shadow stood rigidly without moving, but it became transparent.

"It's the mother's decision and not mine to make."

"*You flatter me, Doctor. She's a mental patient, and you want her to think clearly under the circumstances and make a rational decision? You really want to put this offer into her own hands?*" The demon's laugh filled the room. "*If you think she's capable of deciding, then why haven't you told her about her condition? That she could die during birth? You are a contradiction Doctor, unlike many mortals who believe they provide for the good of man.*"

Dr. Monserrat remained silent as he acknowledged the convincing demon. He paced around the room, curling his hands and twitching his eyes. He'd never had to make a decision like this before, and so he was paralyzed in thought.

He took hold of the gold chain and cross around his neck and kissed it. Then he looked up toward the ominous shadow, eagle-eyed and determined. "Fine, let them live. You'll have the child after ten years, at your discretion and not before then."

He picked up the forceps and threw them to the floor. He was incensed by his decision as he placed his hands over his face, begging forgiveness from God.

Though he was a scientist, he had felt something sinister the first time he had met Abbey. And now, an unborn fetus, on the cuff of choking to death with its umbilical cord wrapped around its neck, had miraculously escaped death.

Delaney came back to the room with the glass of water and placed it on the side table. She quickly attended to Dr. Monserrat, who was in the final stages of delivering a healthy young boy.

Abbey survived the childbirth without complications to her internal organs, despite the odds stacked against her.

As he passed the baby boy to Delaney, he had only one thought, *What in the name of God just happened?*

Would he live to regret the deal he had made with the devil? One thing was for sure—he would never mention a word to anyone about his arrangement with the devil. Not even Dr. Jordan or Abbey.

Dr. Monserrat decided to head off to the abortion

room. He was being pulled to it like a magnet, compelled to confront whatever awaited him. His heightened awareness and sixth sense took over his rational mind. He wanted answers, and he needed them now. Impatient and unprepared to wait, he tried to tackle the evil head-on.

He rushed down the hallway, his white coat flapping in the air like sheets in the wind. One nurse, who was in his way, was brushed aside with barely enough time to dodge him. It was her instinct to jump out of his way before being knocked over by the doctor.

Dr. Monserrat had the master key to the asylum and was entrusted with special access to all the wards. He took his keys from his side pocket and thrust the master key into the lock of the abortion room.

Before he could even settle into his surroundings, the demon lay waiting for him, cross-legged and sitting on the abortion chair. But you would be forgiven to think that the evil entity was anything but a demon—dressed immaculately with the fashion sense of a gentleman. It was poised with a buttoned-up jacket and shirt generally reserved for those who could afford it—the gentry. The demon held his hands together with an inquisitive look, waiting for Dr. Monserrat.

"You're the evil spirit from the delivery room. I sense it."

The demon nodded without saying a word before raising his hands in the air. "A job well done, Doctor. You definitely are the best obstetrician I've seen so far. And better than the one before you—that drunken skunk, Dr. Pendergrass. He would deliver babies with a bottle of the finest scotch whisky in one hand."

"I don't understand you."

"You want to know my purpose and why I'm here?"

Dr. Monserrat nodded while clutching his keys nervously as they rattled from the tension in his hands.

"I'm the child taker; that's what I do. Some demons like to hurt people and tear their limbs apart. Others like to condemn them to suicide. The worst types like to hijack their victims' bodies."

"And you're seeking the souls of children?"

"I like the unborn children for a specific reason. And, despite what you've been taught, the fetus will have a soul at around four months of conception when the spirit knows the mother will go full term. Hmm … So, I like to get them young before they are corrupted by your Christian ways."

"But, what about the health of the mother?"

"A token sacrifice for the child, my dear man. What am I to do with the mother after I obtain the soul of the child? Just another problem I don't need."

Dr. Monserrat stepped sideways to where a large cross was hanging on the wall next to him.

"Do you know the soul of the fetus watches from outside and doesn't enter the womb until it's time? And if a mother aborts the fetus, the soul stays in the energy field, waiting for another opportunity. Suppose this becomes impossible for the soul to be born with this mother. In that case, they either find another female family member or return to spiritual existence and make another plan. Either way, I can't lose, and I eventually get the soul of the child."

Dr. Monserrat disagreed with the demon and wanted to make his point of view. "As for me, I believe a spirit enters the child as soon as it has a heartbeat. I don't believe that the soul decides if the child will live or die before having a soul. I believe that it just goes to that child, and if the child dies, the soul can have another chance at birth again, in another child."

"Oh yes, Doctor, we all have our beliefs, and mine are bound to be different; that's for sure." The demon stood up from the chair and placed his hands on his hips. "But I have to make sure I can get them pregnant first, and this is where you mortals come in handy."

"What do you refer to, demon?"

"Oh, that crazy, sex-crazed, drunken Irishman, Marcus O'Hara, of course. It didn't take me long to get him on board. A crate full of his expensive Irish Cream, and he was off and running like a sex-crazed lunatic."

"We know about O'Hara, the maintenance guy, and we're closing in on him." Dr. Monserrat was putting on a brave face.

"You catch on quick, Doctor. He sows the seed, the women become pregnant, and then comes my souls, untouched by your world, perfect and easily molded into the devil's own. Not a bad system, hey?" He pointed toward Dr. Monserrat as his voice changed into a deep tone, echoing throughout the room. It was a grinding, hoarse voice that sent a chill up the doctor's spine.

"And you think I'm the evil one? The man who graced this room before you, Dr. Pendergrass, his crazy experiments went unnoticed for years. Check your records. He used the women of this asylum as guinea pigs for his experiments on new abortive techniques. Oh, the pain and misery, blood and death that lingers in this room. And the cries of women in abysmal pain, watching their unborn child killed in an unnecessary abortion just to please himself. And you think my world is bad?" The demon nodded, grinning as his sharp fangs penetrated his exalting smile. "There's evil amongst you all, and it's not only reserved for demons. Even you have a touch of the devil. It's just that you don't know about it."

Dr. Monserrat stood silent for a moment as he absorbed the information that the demon had cunningly provided him in a frank manner. "So, why are you telling me all this?"

"I look to cause mayhem, to watch you attack each other professionally. It's the imperfection of man. I want to see what you do with O'Hara. I lost my patience with him when he held me ransom and asked for more riches, greedy bastard." The demon clapped his hands and grinned begrudgingly. "And, who do you think assisted Dr Pendergrass in this room as he performed those horrific acts of debauchery?"

"It was Delaney, wasn't it?"

"Hmm … As I said before, you catch on quickly. She's a monster you know, and has a fetish for the same-sex. Ha-ha." The demon took his cane and raised it, pointing at the wall. "She's the one who cleaned the blood off the walls and floor. And, if you care to look closer, you can see the splattering of the doctor's handiwork. Blood is such a difficult thing to clean from whitewashed walls."

Dr. Monserrat instinctively turned around to inspect the tiny spots of blood that were invisible. He felt the touch of a thorny finger poke him, ice-cold and lifeless. He shook his shoulders, reacting to the sensation, and then turned his head immediately to find the demon was gone from the chair.

"Oh Doctor, as for your proposal to join my ranks, I cannot accommodate it. I respectfully decline."

Dr. Monserrat creased his forehead and squinted his eyes. Then he crossed his arms, looking ahead defiantly at the demon.

"Haven't I made myself clear enough, Doctor?"

The poltergeist faded away, and Dr. Monserrat was left with sobering thoughts.

4 WILLOW COURT ASYLUM

Present Day

Asylums like Willow Court, that once segregated and housed people with disabilities and the mentally ill, laid empty and unused for two decades. Tasmania was the first state in Australia to de-institutionalize all the people it cared for and closed the doors of Willow Court and Royal Derwent Hospital in 2001. Some of the wards had been knocked down to make way for development. Others were still empty, trashed by vandals. The most prominent being Ward C.

A former mental health hospital, Willow Court, had become a drawcard for people who believed in the supernatural. The Derwent Valley Council determined to find out the truth to the stories. Councilors voted in favor of a paranormal investigation in Ward C, the location

50

associated with most paranormal sightings.

Through their contacts, they called on Clarisse Garcia and Harry to lead the investigation. Their reputation in dealing with the supernatural in Hartley and Old Tailem Town had spread around country towns. They were considered the new authority in unraveling mysterious curses that abound around towns.

"We're only about ten minutes away from New Norfolk," Harry said. He had given up his full-time job to be with Clarisse and investigate paranormal events. He was the technical arm of the investigations. He had a passion for state-of-the-art ghostbusting equipment, developed during his time at Hartley. It was something Harry had never imagined he would be doing for a living.

Clarisse clutched her belly that was starting to show. She was six months pregnant, and they were both looking forward to the birth of their first child.

"Bubs just kicked me again," she told him.

"It's more active in the morning than the afternoon?"

"Ha-ha ... Just like you. Hey, Harry?"

Harry shrugged. "I guess so."

They were driving through a misty rain and fog that made visibility poor. Apparently, a typical day in this part of Tasmania.

"So, who are we meeting again?"

"Gary Charlton, the mayor of Derwent Valley Council. He's the guy who contacted us about doing the investigation, remember?"

"Oh yeah. My baby brain again. I keep forgetting things."

Harry shook his head and flicked on the wipers. "It's starting to rain now. It's miserable weather, but it's kind of charming when you blend it in with the surroundings."

"It's nice. I heard New Norfolk is a pretty place."

"Well, don't get too excited. Our investigation hasn't gone down too well with the locals. They're spooked about the whole thing. Some councilors are against having a paranormal investigation and voted against the motion. But the motion passed due to Gary's insistence."

"What do you mean?"

"Gary said some locals are hoping that no evidence of the paranormal is found. Actually, they would prefer if Willow Court's history as an asylum was not dragged up at all."

Clarise nodded and smiled. "It's not the first time we have encountered this mentality. Remember Old Tailem Town? They didn't exactly make it easy for us, did they?"

Harry rolled his eyes. "How could I forget? They did everything to stop us investigating the curse. Some got nasty with us, too."

"Why do you think they're sensitive to our investigation?"

"Gary said some locals have not been keen to admit having a descendant at Willow Court, a family secret often considered sensitive in these parts."

"Well, it was a mental asylum for all those years. I suppose some families have been there for a long time and connected to Willow Court in some way."

Harry nodded then pointed to the sign on the road. "We're only a couple miles out of town." He glanced toward Clarisse and smiled. "I just wanted you to know not to expect a welcoming committee when we get there. The locals don't like what we're doing—waking up the spirits and changing the balance of Willow Court. Best we're prepared for that, right?"

"I get it, Harry—some things are best left alone. Let bygones be bygones. Let sleeping dogs lie."

"Yeah, that's a good way of putting it. Anyway, I've got a surprise when we arrive." Harry put on a cheeky look and raised his eyebrows.

"I've seen that look before, Harry. What is it?"

He paused for a while then let loose. "Do you remember Paranormal Jack Sr. from Hartley?

"How could I forget him? He died so tragically. It was out of the blue and totally unexpected. I liked him a lot.

He was full of personality; always looking at the funny side of things."

"Yeah well, he kind of grew on me too, after a while, and it was sad to see him go like that. But we're meeting his son with the same name."

"What? You're kidding me!"

"Nah, we're meeting Paranormal Jack Jr. He's joining us for the investigation."

"How did they find him?'

"He found us and asked to join our investigation. I didn't think you would have an issue with it."

"Ah … Of course not, Harry. And, if he's anything like his dad, it will be a scream." Clarisse paused for a moment then glanced toward Harry. "But, why didn't you mention it?"

"I wanted to surprise you."

Clarisse nodded. She had become used to Harry's weird sense of humor, although she didn't think it was funny on this occasion. She had a soft spot for Paranormal Jack Sr.

"Looks like we've arrived … New Norfolk. And there's Willow Court over there," she said.

"Still an impressive Colonial building, even though it's been vandalized and not cared for, laid to rot and falling apart." Harry pointed to an older man standing at the entrance of Willow Court. "Oh, Gary is waiting for us."

"Is that Paranormal Jack Jr. next to him?"

"Hmm … You picked it. Looks like his father, doesn't he?"

"Spitting image. Almost like a …"

"Reincarnation?"

"Yeah, something like that. Although, you know I don't believe in reincarnation." Clarisse wanted to make a point.

"Yeah, yeah. Just kidding."

Harry pulled up at the entrance of Willow Court. It was a pebbled driveway that led to the steps of the old colonial structure, made from local quarry stone and crafted by the best artisans in the area. It remained preserved, a testament to how they had built structures in the 1800s—meant to last the test of time.

Gary walked toward the car at a gingerly pace, excited about his new arrivals in town. As the town mayor, he was the one who had pushed at the council meetings to hold a paranormal investigation and deliver the findings to the subcommittee. A man in his late fifties, his family had lived in New Norfolk for generations. So, like most of the residents, he was connected somehow.

Harry stepped out of the car then assisted Clarisse, who found stepping out from her seat challenging.

Gary put his hand out for a solid handshake and greeted Harry with the usual Aussie charm. "Nice to meet ya in person, Harry, and thanks again for accepting my invitation." He looked toward Clarisse and smiled. "Hello, miss. So, you're the one they call the spirit hunter?"

Clarisse smiled and nodded in acknowledgment. Gary reminded her of their time in Old Tailem Town and dealing with the local folk. Most of them had a down-to-earth, casual, and friendly demeanor, and Gary was no different.

"I see you're pregnant, luv?" Gary raised his eyebrows and tightened his lips.

"Yes, six months, and I'm starting to feel the child kick. It moves around a lot more."

Gary laughed. He took an immediate liking to Clarisse. "There are some stories about infant ghosts that have been haunting Willow Court for over a hundred years, but we can talk about that later when I brief you on the assignment."

"She's not easily frightened, Gary," Harry said with a smirk on his face.

"Oh, good on ya, Harry. I like a man with a sense of humor. How about I introduce Paranormal Jack Jr., waiting at the steps over there. He's keen to meet you both since you knew his father?"

"Oh yeah, his dad joined us for our investigation in Hartley." Harry looked toward Paranormal Jack Jr. and waved. "He's the spitting image of his father, isn't he?"

Clarisse agreed, nodding her head. "It's like déjà vu. He smiles and dresses like him, too." She pointed to him and said, "And that's Paranormal Jack's hat."

"You're right. How could we miss that bushman's hat?"

"You've got some great equipment in the Ute, mate," Paranormal Jack Jr. called out as they walked toward him. He was wearing the black bushman's hat, his long, black, shoulder-length hair thrown about in the wind. He wasn't a fashion statement, but he certainly looked the part of a typical home-grown country boy.

Harry smiled as he walked toward Paranormal Jack Jr. and shook his hand firmly as he looked into his eyes. "You look like your father, you know. And I got to thank him for getting me into ghostbusting technology. Otherwise, I'd still be working as a communications engineer."

"Everyone said we looked like twins. And yeah, Dad was into the technology big time. Always coming home with something new." Paranormal Jack Jr. pointed to the Ute. "So, what do you have in there?"

"We've got voice recorders to capture electronic voice phenomena, including static or stray noises. We've got electromagnetic field meters to capture any presence. Cameras and temp guns for temperature readings to work out if there are any temperature spikes or drops," Harry said with an exuberant tone in his voice.

"Hmm ... That's the best equipment I've ever seen, and Dad would have been impressed. You really know your stuff, Harry."

He waved to Clarisse and smiled. "So, that's the spirit hunter my father wouldn't stop talking about. All I could ever hear was Clarisse this and Clarisse that. It was all about her connections with the spirit world."

"He told you that?"

"Yeah, many times before he died."

"Come and meet Clarisse, then. She's keen to say hello. Oh, and by the way, she had a soft spot for your dad, and his death affected her," Harry whispered.

Paranormal Jack Jr. nodded in acknowledgment. He was aware of Clarisse and his father's spiritual bond in Hartley Town while hunting down the curse.

As they walked toward the car, a gust of wind blew across the street, capturing everyone by surprise. And although it was misty, and some low-level fog lay on the surface of the road, it was a calm day. Leaves flew in the air as they picked up the dust from the pebble driveway.

Clarisse stopped instinctively and looked straight at the entrance of Willow Court. She felt a kick more than once. Her child was unusually active for this time of day.

"What is it, Clarisse?" Harry asked.

She clutched her belly and placed her hand on it, rubbing it in a circular motion. "I've never felt the baby react this way ... It's stressed."

"Oh, it's just the long drive to get here. Being positioned in a car for so long. It's probably nothing."

"You think so?"

"Yeah, nothing to worry about, Clarisse."

"Oh, it's really agitated, Harry. There's another kick." Clarisse continued looking at the entrance of Willow Court, squinting as she tried to focus her eyes. She felt a tingling sensation in her back. It started mildly in her lower back then gradually moved up her spine to her neck, as though someone was rolling their fingers across it. She shook and twisted her back, creating an intense lock in her muscles. It wasn't painful, but it was a sensation she recognized—the devil's touch of a spirit awakened and wanting to communicate. Then a bony finger poked her in the shoulder blade, causing her to rattle her arm uncontrollably.

Harry watched on, unsure what was going in. "Are you feeling something sinister, Clarisse?"

"It was a vibration from a dead spirit trying to get my attention. It came from the building."

"You've felt this before, haven't you?" Harry had seen her react like this during other demonic encounters with dead spirits and poltergeists. Clarisse could latch on to the vibration of a spirit entity and communicate with them between the realms of death and immortality. She was a beacon for the spirit world that had not transitioned to the afterlife. Clarisse was their guiding light and watch post, a symbol of hope to salvage them from the dangers that riddled their world. That was why they latched on to her, so she could lead them to find peace.

"Hmm ... Let's go to the motel, Harry, and get ready for the briefing at midday." As Clarisse turned to the car parked directly in front of them, she noticed a dark shadow from the corner of her eye race across the main window of Willow Court. It was followed by a flicker of white light. Then a gentle giggle of a fastidious child tapped into her hearing spectrum. It lasted only a couple of seconds, and it would have been lost to anyone else, but Clarisse was not an average person with a heightened sense of spiritual awareness. Triggers like that meant something to her. They were snippets of time that led to paranormal sightings. It was a form of drip-feed from whoever was in the building, to signal their intent or warn her away.

"Did you hear that giggle, Harry?"

"No, Clarisse. Maybe it's the wind whistling between the building and the trees."

They waved to Paranormal Jack Jr. and Gary as they

stepped inside the car. But that was not all …

Standing in a black outfit, with his hands in his pockets, was an elderly priest. His receding white hair flickered in the wind as he looked on emotionlessly. Clarisse wasn't the focus of his attention, though. He was fixated on the entrance to Willow Court. Stoic and stiff, like a statue, he barely moved in the stiff breeze or blinked an eyelid. Something had caught his attention and drawn him to that spot. The priest didn't appear spooked or uncomfortable, as though he had seen it before and knew what to expect.

"I haven't seen a priest wear a white collar for a long time," Clarisse said as she adjusted her seat belt to allow for the expansion of her belly.

Harry shrugged while he slammed the car door shut and turned on the ignition. "He's probably the traditional type, and he looks old. You know, this is a sleepy town, tucked away from everything, and things move slowly around here."

"Yeah, I keep forgetting we're not living in the city anymore. It's a lot easier to keep your ways and traditions in quiet country towns like this. We saw the same at Hartley and Old Tailem Town—people stick to their old ways."

Before Harry drove off, he took a notebook from the car's glove box and flicked the pages until he found what he was looking for. "Here it is … Saint Peter's church, New Norfolk."

Clarisse chuckled. "I can always rely on you to do your homework, Harry—checking over the detail before we arrive."

Harry grinned and read from his notebook.

"St Peter's Catholic Church was built on land granted by the government in 1864, following approaches by Bishop R.W. Wilson. When the foundation stone was finally laid by Bishop Murphy in 1885, over 1000 people turned out to witness the historic occasion. They came from as far away as Hamilton, Brighton & Richmond."

He looked toward Clarisse while closing the notebook and placing it on the dashboard. "See? A historic church that had its foundation way back to the convict settlement era. Lots of history there."

Clarisse nodded and threw her hands in the air. "Yeah, I can always rely on you for the info dump." She pointed to the road. "Can we pass by the church on the way to the motel? I'm curious now."

Harry pressed on the accelerator as he gently skidded on the pebbled driveway toward the main road, leaving a puff of smoke behind his trail.

"It's just a couple of minutes up the road. I think we passed it on the way in, but it was misty and hard to see."

Clarisse glanced to her side to find a small unit, the size of a mobile phone. It was flashing green and red lights. She had never seen it before.

"What's this?" she asked, picking it up and attempting to flick on the switch.

"Oh, don't touch that, Clarisse. You'll erase the recording."

She frowned in confusion while staring at Harry. "Are you recording me?"

"No, don't be silly. It's a surprise."

"What do you mean? This box is a surprise? How?"

Harry shrugged while taking the box from her. "It's my new spirit device. I wanted to surprise you with it."

"Hmm …"

"Yes, Clarisse, I had it built specifically for our paranormal investigation at Willow Court. It's been a year in the making, and finally, this is the working prototype." Harry turned on a switch with his left hand while holding the steering wheel with the other, one eye on the road and the other on the spirit device. "When you turn on this switch, it scans the room for frequencies that aren't within our range, and that our ears can't pick up."

"Yeah, I know spirits communicate on different frequencies, and we haven't discovered all of them yet. Each spirit can be different than the other, which makes communicating really hard." She pointed to the front of the road. "Do you think you can concentrate on your driving? I'm pregnant, you know."

Harry placed the spirit box into a compartment then took a hold of the wheel with both hands. "That's right; and wouldn't it be great to pick up the sounds of spirits that we haven't been able to before, to communicate more effectively and find out what they want?"

"Well yeah, that's one of my biggest frustrations. I get some signals and sometimes none. And it annoys the hell out of me because I sense their presence."

"They're there all right, but you can't hear them, see them, or feel them. It's like screaming through soundproof glass, and the person on the other side hasn't a clue you're there." Harry took a sharp right into the road leading to Saint Peter's church; however, he couldn't stop boasting about the spirit box. "It's based on a series of spiritual vibrations from low to high frequencies, and it's staggering how many I was able to construct."

Clarisse smiled and patted Harry on the arm. "You're always full of surprises. I can't wait to use it at Willow Court."

"Talking of surprises … you know when you sensed something at Willow Court? A presence or a giggle of a child?"

"No way! You didn't?"

"I recorded it. That was my surprise."

"Did you get something, Harry?"

"We shall see. I'll play it back to you when we stop at Saint Peter's."

Clarisse lay back in her seat and sighed, looking directly at the road in front of her as the sandstone building of Saint Peter's came into view.

The building had been completed in 1887. It was designed by renowned Hobart architect, Henry Hunter, and constructed by John Thurley of New Norfolk. The sandstone used during the construction had been quarried from the properties of locals. It was in excellent condition and had been renovated by the Catholic Archdiocese.

As they got closer to the church, Clarisse took an immediate liking to its charm and presence. Behind the church was the presbytery, flanked by manicured roses.

Harry stopped the car in front of the church and wound down their windows.

"That can't be the same priest from Willow Court?" Clarisse pointed to the ominous black outline of a man standing on the steps of the presbytery. The mist that had formed over the town made it difficult to get a clear view from where they were parked.

"It's probably another priest of the same age. I don't think he could have returned here so quickly." Harry squinted while, at the same time, tried to look composed so as not to upset her.

"I wish I could get a closer look, but maybe another day," she said.

Harry closed the windows then took the spirit box from the glove box. "Do you want to hear what we captured at Willow Court?"

"I almost forgot about that. Of course, Harry. Let's see what you got. I'm so curious."

Harry flicked on the audio switch then played back the recording. "It's the first time I've tested it in a real situation."

A crackle of interference lasted for about ten seconds, followed by a static sound, the same as adjusting the dial of an old-style radio to lock in on a station's signal. It was followed by the voice of a child, a young boy of no more than eight years old. It was the sound of innocence; so pure and polite that you just wanted to hug the infant in your arms, such was its magnetism.

At first, it was difficult to make out the words, but then it became more apparent. Harry had built a new feature to remove noises that were associated with another dimension. They distorted and interfered with the voices of the spirit world, and Harry worked out a way to separate the vibrations.

"*Come play with me … Come on; come play with me.*"

But then came the sound of an older girl, maybe around twelve years of age.

"*Come play in the playground … Come, come.*"

And then a boy of approximately five years old; a squeakier voice with a broken sentence.

"*Do you want to play ball? Kick the ball?*"

You could have been mistaken to associate the voices with kids playing in a local park.

Clarisse was silent, absorbed by the captivating, pure essence of the children's voices.

Harry shook his head more than once, having expected a more sinister, demonic front than infants' gentle, inspiring sounds.

"Surely you've tuned into the voices of a kindergarten nearby," Clarisse said. It was a strange comment coming from a spirit hunter; one of disbelief.

Harry shrugged, thinking he was usually the skeptical one. "I don't recall seeing a kindergarten next to the church, and anyway, the spirit device has been set to filter out human voices. Notice that it never picked up on our conversations?"

Clarisse paused for a moment. Never one to rush her responses, she clasped her hands together and brushed her hair aside. "Yeah, that makes sense. Now I sound like the skeptical one."

"It's okay. They're children and have innocent voices. That's enough to give anyone the chills."

Harry turned on the ignition and fastened his seat belt while Clarisse turned away, looking forward toward the church for another look. She wanted to be sure no children were playing nearby.

Tap, tap, tap.

"Ah!" She raised her hands in the air and screamed, as though confronted by an unwelcome poltergeist in a dark cavern.

A gentle tap on the window caught her attention, followed by the image of the same priest who they had seen at Willow Court.

He tapped a few times again until Clarisse got the courage to wind down the window. A white receding hairline and pointed nose that seemed to poke out from a narrow face greeted her. The priest smiled with broken, yellow teeth and sharp, aging lines along the contours of his eyes.

"Sorry to startle you like that, miss. I tried waving from

afar as I approached the car, but you were both in conversation." He nodded and blinked with his right eye. "I'm Father O'Connor of Saint Peter's church that you see in front of you, and you must be the girl everyone in town is talking about, the spirit hunter?"

Clarisse took a deep breath and attempted to lower her pulse rate and reduce her heart palpitations. "Hello, Father. Do you always sneak up on people like that? It was almost stealth-like. I never saw you coming until you tapped on the window."

Father O'Connor adjusted his white collar and smiled. "I'm a priest. I don't think anyone ever sees me coming. And this is your partner?"

"Oh yes Father, meet Harry. We work together now on paranormal investigations."

Harry waved without saying a word, preferring to let Clarisse do all the talking.

"They talked about the paranormal investigation at the local community meeting after the council approved your research. But not all the locals are happy, so I thought it best to let you know in advance. You may get the cold shoulder from some of those who have past family members connected to the asylum. We're a small, tight knit community, you know."

"Sure, Father. Your mayor told us about the feeling

around the place. It's not lost on us. We have actually seen it before in other ghost towns."

"Like Hartley?"

"You know about that?"

"Oh yes," Father O'Connor said, his facing brimming with knowledge. "I think everyone knows what happened there. A one-hundred-and-fifty-year-old curse and how you released the town from its evil past."

"We've been traveling a long time to get here, Father," Harry said, having kept the engine running throughout the conversation, hoping Father O'Connor would walk away. "Perhaps we can catch up tomorrow after we have rested?"

"Oh yes, of course. How inconsiderate of me. Let's talk tomorrow, if you get time. That's my place over there, the presbytery. I've lived here for forty years, you know."

"I think we can make time to visit Father O'Connor tomorrow, Harry?

"Sure, Clarisse. I'm sure Father O'Connor has a lot of history and stories to tell us about Willow Court Asylum." Harry was tired from his travel to New Norfolk and was at the stage where he would agree to anything if he could get some rest and something to eat.

Father O'Connor blushed uncomfortably, as though he was under stress and holding back on his discomfort. He clutched the cross around his neck and said, "Oh yes,

Willow Court … stories abound about that place. Not sure how much the mayor filled you in, but I'm sure I can cover the missing pieces. Huh, who knows, after an hour with me, you might change your mind about your paranormal investigation? But don't let an old, worn-down priest like me frighten you."

Harry looked directly at Clarisse, as though they were both ready to unleash on each other. They had only been in New Norfolk for a couple of hours and sensed the town was steeped in superstition, locked in a battle of fear. Its past was ingrained amongst the locals through their connection with Willow Court. And, like most country towns with historical cases of poltergeist encounters, the locals preferred to not ruffle the feathers of the evil that roamed the town for over a century.

That was why the local council had passed a motion to get to the bottom of it. And, although Gary had lived in New Norfolk for generations, he was also regarded as a maverick. As mayor, he was not afraid to push the pendulum a little further to the right and deal with the town's obsession with the mental asylum for the damned.

It was a Colonial-rich past that was layered by scandal, debauchery, and maltreatment of patients. Nobody had cared what had gone on behind those four walls until babies died unexplainably, and the media latched on to it in 1878 with headlines, like:

A Cluster of Babies Found Dead at Willow Court!

There had been four babies altogether—two boys and two girls, of which one baby was found barely alive and survived.

The locals said the town had become cursed, and the devil had taken refuge amongst the patients at Willow Court. The asylum had become associated with superstition, demonic possession, and evil. But, if it stayed within those four walls, the residents accepted it, though reluctantly.

They took precautions by placing objects at their doorsteps, underneath chimneys, doors, and windows, to ensure the evil presence was locked out of their homes. Children were deemed the most vulnerable, particularly the younger ones of elementary school age.

The local church, Saint Peter's, fostered this belief during mass, making sure that prayers to the souls of the damned at Willow Court were included. If the prayers were strong enough, then the spiritual power of the many could push away the evil spirits, preventing them from entering their homes. And these prayers that started over a century were maintained during mass—*The Prayer for the Damned.*

The beliefs at New Norfolk were found ingrained in the culture amongst the locals. And, while Gary had been successful in sponsoring a paranormal investigation, they felt he had underestimated the power of the evil that resided within Willow Court. The locals feared a rebirth of the demonic encounters that dated back to 1870's. The cluster of babies found dead had become part of the local folklore.

As had been said, it was not that Harry and Clarisse hadn't encountered this mood before in a small town. They had been bereft of such feeling in Hartley and Old Tailem Town. But there was something different when a Catholic priest believed in the local superstition and warned against their investigation.

Plus, when the mayor, who had sponsored the paranormal investigation, also expressed caution that the mood in the town was not supportive of their actions, it begged to question why they had bothered with a controversial inquiry in the first place. Poking the unknown while unlocking dark secrets would open old wounds. A cluster of babies found dead in 1878 would be the precursor to investigating Willow Court Asylum and its shady history.

5 PARANORMAL INVESTIGATIONS

Paranormal Jack Jr., Clarisse, and Harry met with Gary Charlton at the council office to brief the paranormal investigations.

"So, I'm going to give you instructions for the paranormal investigation. Unfortunately, it's not that straightforward, and you won't have free rein in the whole facility. It's one of the trade-offs that I had to make with the councilors to get it approved," Gary told them.

"You've got some superstitious councilors?" Paranormal Jack Jr. asked. He was a straight shooter like his dad and didn't mince words.

Gary rested back in his seat and took a sip of his freshly brewed coffee. "Yeah, you know what it's like in old country towns, especially those early settlements that didn't make their fortunes in gold mining. This town was used as a service center for the colonial settlement in Hobart. Lots of convicts passed through this place with all sorts of criminal records. And you know where the insane ones ended up? Willow Court Asylum."

Paranormal Jack Jr. nodded, as he found the historical context interesting.

Gary placed a document on the table and pointed to the first page. "This is your brief. A team of three from the Paranormal Investigation Unit will plan a three-night stay in Ward C that once housed the criminally insane."

"Is that it?" Harry asked.

"Yep, simple and sweet. We're not complicated people like your city folk who require a ten-page report." Gary smiled as he handed Harry the keys to Ward C and a detailed map of the ward. "The drawings are old, but they're still relevant; nothing has changed at Willow Court for decades."

"We have lots of equipment, and we need power," Harry prompted.

"That's been done. A power line from the street was organized last week with a power point fixed in Ward C. You can run extension cables from there. It was all part of the approval for costs included in the plan for the council." Gary took a deep breath then sipped on his coffee again. "Oh, and here is the emergency beeper that communicates to the local police and fire brigade."

"Do we really need that?" Paranormal Jack Jr. asked.

"It's an old building, and while you're in there, we need to care for your safety, including fire regulations. Again, another requirement from the council." Gary placed the beeper on the table in front of them. "I had an inspection completed last week and cleared the trash from the squatters we found occupying the place. We had them forcibly removed."

"Squatters?" Harry asked.

"Yeah, they come and go. We know who they are—homeless youth who don't want help, rebels who keep getting dragged into Ward C." Gary put his hands over his mouth and whispered, "I never told you this, but they look like demons—dress in black, demonic tattoos all over, pitch-black hair, dark eyeliner—that sort of stuff."

Harry nodded in acknowledgment. "They sound like a weird lot."

"Tell me something, and just for my own knowledge; what's the difference between a ghost, poltergeist, and a demon?" Gary was curious about the paranormal investigation to the point that he had started his own research on spirit entities. "It was a question raised by one of the councilors, and I had no idea how to respond."

Everyone turned to Clarisse, expecting her to answer.

Clarisse leaned forward and clasped her hands together. "Well, where ghosts, poltergeists, and demons are concerned, they are all very different. Ghosts are the least bothersome. They can make spooky noises and be a general nuisance, but that's it. They can't pick up objects and move them. They pass through doors, etc. Ghosts can be seen as misty apparitions. They are usually the spirits of people who have died but haven't crossed over. It could be that they don't want to leave their loved ones, or maybe there's unfinished business they need to take care of. Perhaps they just weren't ready to die. They usually gravitate toward a particular home, or a town that's important to them.

"Poltergeists are troublesome spirits who will haunt a particular person. They are usually mischievous—making objects move. They can bite, pinch, physically attack, throw objects, and break things. They can't be seen, just like ghosts." Clarisse took a deep breath and adjusted her posture in the chair. "Poltergeists are more of a force field or kinetic energy that feed directly into the emotional state of a particular person. They are very rarely linked to any given place or location. They can levitate things, like people, furniture, etc. They are most usually violent and classified as extremely dangerous.

"Demons are the really naughty guys. They are a malevolent evil that can take over a person's body, causing irreparable damage. They've been classified as fallen angels. They can be extremely persuasive and make a person kill. They prey on those who are emotionally troubled, too weak to make decisions for themselves, and who can't think clearly."

Clarisse paused and took another deep breath before sipping her bottle of water. "There's another form, as well. You may or may not have heard about ectoplasm, a substance or spiritual energy that surrounds ghosts. It's usually light in color and exudes from the body of a spirit medium in a trance-like state, usually in a darkened atmosphere. It can take the shape of a hand, face, or a complete body, and it usually disappears at the end of a seance."

"*Phew* … That's a handful, but I get it now. What do you expect to find—a ghost, poltergeist or, dare I say, a demon?" Gary squinted, looking directly at Clarisse.

"Hmm … That's always the million-dollar question, Gary. We don't know until we see the type of manifestations … if any. Only then can we get an understanding of the spirit entity that has taken hold at Willow Court."

"Yes, I see. That makes perfect sense. Well, here is my card with my personal mobile number. If you need anything, let me know. You can get started with your investigation as soon as you're ready. I've asked the local fire chief to help you get inside and settle in; show you where the power supply is. He also has food and water supplies for a couple of days."

"You've really prepared this well," Harry commented.

"Yeah, it's been an ongoing project of mine for a year now, so we've had plenty of time to organize ourselves. Plus, our council requested updates at every meeting."

"Oh, and one question before we leave."

"Sure, Harry, what's on your mind?"

"I did some research on Ward C and Willow Court ..." Harry paused for a moment as he tried to phrase the question, as to not sound provocative. "Isn't Ward C where the abortion room is located? Apparently, the abortion chair is intact and preserved."

"That's right."

"And I read there was a doctor who worked in the ward. His name was Dr. Monserrat, and he wrote a report on his findings at the time ... 1878 or thereabouts."

Gary creased his forehead, and his eyes twitched. "I think that's about right, too."

"Apparently, a cluster of babies died mysteriously during childbirth, and they were found by a Dr. Jordan, head physician at the time. He stated abortions were performed illegally, a type of illegal experimentation."

"Yes." Gary looked at his watch erratically. "Oh, time to go. Sorry, we need to continue this conversation later on."

"Witnesses have heard sounds of young children playing in Ward C. Sometimes they can be heard outside Willow Court." Harry was being persistent, not wanting to let Gary off the hook.

"Are you going to answer his question?" a very forceful Paranormal Jack Jr. asked.

Gary hesitated then stood up. "I don't want to prejudice the paranormal investigations with my thoughts on what's in there. If there is indeed a presence, let's see what you find." Gary walked to the door to lead them out. "Got some council business to get to. I wish you well with your investigation, and we'll catch up for an update on your progress."

Clarisse took hold of Harry's arm, encouraging him to leave. He knew the cue and obliged.

Clarisse had become uncomfortable with Gary and sensed he was hiding something. As for Paranormal Jack Jr., he felt he had achieved his objective—constantly pushing people for more information and taking them out of their comfort zone.

Once they were outside, Gary closed the door to his office with a *bang*.

Clarisse turned to Harry with her hands on her hips. "So, you going to tell us more about this Dr. Monserrat? Oh, and by the way, thanks for letting me know beforehand."

Paranormal Jack Jr. grinned and patted him on the shoulder. "That was very impromptu. We didn't see it coming, especially Gary."

"Do you really have the report by the doctor?" Clarisse was becoming impatient.

Harry stood silently, not sure how to respond. "Well yes, I managed to get hold of it."

"And …?"

"Clarisse, there's stuff that went on at Willow Court that I don't think you want to know about." Harry looked directly at her pregnant belly and frowned.

"It's that bad?"

"Let me put it this way; it made me sick to my stomach." He pointed toward the exit of the local council offices and continued walking.

"Tell me Harry. I really want to know," Clarisse insisted.

Paranormal Jack Jr. nodded likewise. "Go on. Tell us, mate."

Harry sighed and reluctantly agreed. "It was 1878, and Dr. Monserrat was the obstetrician at the asylum. He attended to mentally ill patients who inexplicably got pregnant. However, it was Dr. Jordan who was the head of the asylum. It says in the report that a cluster of newborn babies were mysteriously found by Dr. Jordan—four of them altogether, with no known cause. Only one child was found barely alive and survived. But, other strange things, such as illegal abortions and experiments on unborn fetuses, were found to have taken place. That's why they called it the abortion room."

Clarisse gulped while Paranormal Jack Jr. remained expressionless.

"But there's more. The maintenance man was a rapist, and the head nurse physically abused the mentally ill patients. She was rumored to like women of the same sex, and it was all part of a coordinated effort between them. If you ask me, it was triage of evil that roamed that place for years."

"The maintenance man was sexually abusing women while the head nurse turned a blind eye to ensure she got her fetish?" Paranormal Jack Jr. questioned.

"Yep, that's pretty much the conclusion in his report." Harry paused for a moment and took a deep breath. "The most interesting part of his report was about the devil roaming Ward C. He believed the asylum was under the influence of an evil entity who preyed on mothers and their unborn children. The staff had become superstitious, and the patients started resorting to old rituals to ward off the evil."

"What sort of rituals?" Clarisse prompted.

"It was the superstitious kind. They found objects underneath chimneys, doors, and windows to ward off the evil spirits—crosses, toys, clothing. The staff wore chains with crosses and evil eyes to protect themselves."

"So, whatever happened to Dr. Monserrat?"

"Hmm … This is the irony. Instead of taking heed of the report and acting on it, his superiors concluded he was losing his mind and transferred him to Hobart. And with that, his report was tucked away into the archives for over a century."

"Until you managed to scoop it up," Paranormal Jack Jr. said with a larrikin smile.

Harry nodded. "It's what I do best—investigate the paranormal and look for facts to support our work."

"Huh, and he does it very well," Clarisse said with a smile.

Paranormal Jack Jr. patted Harry on the back. "I guess that's what makes you both such a formidable investigating team."

His father, Paranormal Jack Sr., had considered Harry

a skeptic in Hartley. He had taken him on a challenge to the local cemetery at midnight with ghostbusting equipment to show him the paranormal side of the town. Harry had never been the same and had become attuned to the spirit world. Aware there was more to life than our own everyday being, Harry had learned that most people were two-dimensional in their thinking, shutting off the spirit world around them. He had decided to open to the spirit world by improving his self-awareness and being attuned to the possibility they existed.

Harry and Paranormal Jack Sr. had hit it off as friends after their night in the cemetery and before his sudden death. He admired Paranormal Jack Jr. for showing the same qualities as his father. It was reminiscent of their short time together at Hartley.

Clarisse had a soft spot for Paranormal Jack Jr., realizing his sense of enthusiasm and strength of character. They would form a trio of investigators, ready to enter the spirit world of Ward C, backed up by the best ghostbusting equipment and seasoned spirit hunters in the country.

But the audio recording on the spirit box that Harry had played back to her alluded to one thing—the infant spirits knew Clarisse was in town, and they had attempted to communicate to her in their frequency. Their vibration, as Harry would describe it technically, was no fluke. It was an invitation, but also a trap. What else could be more inviting than the sweet sounds of children laughing and playing, exuberating their charismatic, gentle voices, full of hope and playfulness, for a soon-to-be mother who was six months pregnant?

It triggered a rush of emotion, and Clarisse wanted to know more.

Her view was always that spirits in transition could be saved from their current existence if she connected and showed them the way out. Sometimes, that was all it took. But that meant getting the spirit to trust you and realize their mortality. It had to be a nurturing process with children's souls, because they behaved like children even though they were dead. It was all part of Clarisse's approach to determine the proper connection to make.

Clarisse understood from previous investigations that children didn't act alone. They were led by an entity more powerful and with a vested interest; a more sinister objective. The children served a purpose, yet she was unsure of their role at Willow Court Asylum.

Dr. Monserrat had sought to discover what had led to the curse and had failed due to the prevailing attitudes at the time. His forward-thinking manner would have been unacceptable to those in authority. They would have said he was a brash young doctor who needed a good dose of reality and institutionalization. It was a tragic story of someone willing to make changes but was stifled.

This meant the evil at Willow Court Asylum had continued to flourish, supported by those willing to harbor it for their own deviant ways.

Clarisse understood that every demon that occupied a place or building could not act alone. They needed the intervention of mortals as a go-between.

This was how Delaney had become influential, and O'Hara with his wicked ways. The devil had used them to perform its dirty work, because they were weak in the mind and prone to corruption. It hadn't taken much to convince them to carry out his dirty deeds. With their help, the devil could infiltrate the mothers and children of the asylum to achieve its cursed ways.

6 WARD C

It was mid-afternoon, and the mist hadn't cleared in New Norfolk. The temperature had dropped below ten degrees, and there was an uncomfortable chill in the air. There was no wind, but a morbid stillness. It was as though time stood frozen in this historic, rural town.

Harry and Paranormal Jack Jr. were in front of the temporary steel fencing to stop vandals and squatters from breaking into Ward C. It was partially effective, but anyone with a bit of smarts would have discovered gaps in the perimeter fencing, enough to slip through. Harry could see a pothole dug to slide underneath the fence in a desperate attempt to find shelter. Nevertheless, it was more of a deterrent than anything else.

It was a brave act indeed, if you really put your mind to it, considering many squatters got the fright of their life and left the asylum screaming after their evil encounter. But nobody believed them, let alone the police, who could have charged them for trespassing, instead.

But it wasn't the squatters trashing the place that upset the locals; it had more to do with disturbing the infant spirits that were believed to roam the ward at night. Was it just local superstition, or was there some truth to it? That was up to the paranormal investigative team to find out and provide evidence.

"I'd be lying to you if I said I don't feel creeped-out about this place," Paranormal Jack Jr. said, thrusting his key into the rusty padlock that barely held the entrance gates together.

Harry looked on patiently as Paranormal Jack Jr. removed the padlock and pushed the gates open with a big kick of his cowboy boots. "Yeah, it's got an uneasy feeling about it."

"Huh, you don't feel welcome, mate? They're only ghosts. I'm sure you can handle it." Paranormal Jack Jr. was his usual self—a sarcastic joker who liked to poke fun at anyone.

Harry shrugged, as he was more captured by his personality than his remarks. It reminded him of his time in the graveyard at Hartley with his father. Paranormal Jack Sr. would joke about the spirit world for a bit of fun. The larrikin in him had been passed onto his son, and Harry kind of liked that in Paranormal Jack Jr.

"It's what I would expect your dad to say to me, Jack. Like father like son?"

Paranormal Jack Jr. stopped dead in his tracks and pondered. "I do miss him a lot, you know. He was always cracking a joke about something that happened during his ghost tours."

Paranormal Jack Jr. pointed to the main entrance to Willow Court Asylum. The doors were still in their original, solid, mahogany style and unchanged for over a century. It was a building made of solid red brick with a porch entrance that spanned the entire front of the building. Many Georgian-style windows lined the building in what was an early attempt at mental health care reengineering.

Gone were those dreary caged rooms where any trickle of light or familiarity with the outside environment was considered unnecessary. The draconian way of looking after mental patients had taken a revolutionary turn for an inventive approach—new techniques, behaviors, and surroundings designed for rehabilitation. Willow Court Asylum was built as a refuge for enlightenment. Social engineering would ensure mental health patients recovered then assimilated into the community. It was an experiment that had proven to be a failure in the end, but the building reflected the early enthusiasm of such a project embedded in its design.

The social experiment had failed not because of the efforts of doctors who had managed the project, but because the locals didn't want mental patients assimilating in their community. The wealthy families who had paid for the care of family members hadn't wanted to expose their chink in the armor. There had been a prevailing attitude to keep their mentally sick family members out of sight, and caring for mental patients from home had not been an option back then.

"I suppose I should start bringing the equipment while you make your way inside. I'll back up the Ute so we don't have to carry the stuff too far. Easier on the muscles, right?" Harry blinked as he handed Paranormal Jack Jr. the spirit box.

"What's this nifty little device, mate?"

"Just had it made. It's a spirit box unlike any other—hundreds of new vibrations. If there's anything in there, I guarantee it will pick it up."

Paranormal Jack Jr. took the spirit box from Harry like a boy with a new toy. "I suppose I just press this button, and I'm up and running?"

Harry nodded and smiled, having known perfectly well

that he was going to be excited by the new device. "Go for it. Have a bit of fun." He gave him the thumbs-up then made his way to the Ute parked in the pebbled driveway.

Paranormal Jack Jr. opened the door to the main entrance of Willow Court, and it was not what he had expected to find. In his own imagination, he had thought of a dreary, narrow, bending type of structure, synonymous with mental institutions at the time. However, he was greeted by a vast, open, expansive foyer, like a grand hotel.

Parts of the roof had fallen in, and the large architraves around the doors were chipped, with paint peeling off to the raw timber. The original limestone-colored walls were still apparent, although faded in parts. It had been an attempt to create a more positive and vibrant ambiance. Instead of the dull, smokey, white-washed walls associated with most asylums, Willow Court was considered progressive. The colors they had chosen were evident of this thinking.

Ten doors flanked either side of the hallway, leading to rooms that would have housed the patients separately rather than in shared accommodation. Ward C was more grandiose, with better facilities than the other wards. Those not so lucky to be sponsored by a wealthy family had to accept less favorable surroundings and facilities in different wards.

Each room told a story of a patient—their lives and tribulations as they struggled with being shunned by their families in the name of mental health care.

To have been diagnosed with a mental health issue back then had also meant superstition to the families. The possibility that a demon had taken over their souls because of their weak minds or an opportunistic encounter. For this reason, the church also had a hand in the welfare of the patients, and Saint Peter's had never been too far away, monitoring the interest of patients in a futile attempt to cleanse their souls from evil. But the church was also protecting the spread of evil into the community—at least, that was the thinking at the time.

Although it had been an asylum of the state, Paranormal Jack Jr. could see the outlines of the holy cross on the walls—the church's influence at the time. The institutions were inseparable; you could not run a mental asylum without the involvement of the church in some capacity

A large corridor, with doors on either side, circled a curved staircase, leading to a basement in the middle of the hallway. A broken-down sign lay at the foot of the stairs with a warning not to enter.

What's down there? he thought.

Underground basements always contained surprises and evidence of paranormal activity, so he knew it would become a place of interest. It was the perfect environment for evil entities to hide away.

Locked behind the solid mahogany door lay a basement that nobody had frequented for decades. The door was too big and cumbersome to be broken into by squatters, who were not ingenious enough or too frightened to check out the underground room.

His curiosity getting the better of him, Paranormal Jack Jr. decided to walk down the stairs that led to the mahogany door.

The stairs creaked with each step but were solid, a testament to the craftsmanship of the time. As he approached the door, he felt an uneasy sense of despair, as though sadness had fallen upon him; a change in mood that suddenly came about without warning. He noticed old scratch marks on the door that appeared as though someone had desperately tried to get in. Was it from a battle with an evil entity?

They were fine lines of protrusion that could only have been done by a sharp object. Piercing, nail-like scratches that must have come from an animal with long claws. A mountain lion or a bear? They were not human scratches, that was obvious.

He rubbed his hands over the door in a circular motion, although it didn't serve any practical purpose. He could feel the indentation of the scratches, and when he placed his hand over them, it matched the outline of a giant hand—five scratches, within equal distance of each other, forming the template of the devil's paw.

But that was the difference between Paranormal Jack Jr. and other ghost investigators—like Clarisse, he could feel his way through houses by picking up paranormal vibrations and energy sources. It was a skill he had learned from his dad while leveraging off his spiritual awareness. In most cases, it was something you were born with.

He rubbed his hand over the door once more as he latched on to a sinister vibration. Was it a message from the dark world or a warning?

He closed his eyes and focused on the energy field that was pulling him toward the door, and as he did so, flashes of images crossed his mind like a slideshow at fast speed.

A pregnant woman bleeding from her belly that had been cut open while the hand of a fetus stuck out. More screams and a plea for help. Her face washed with pain and anger. Then a dead fetus on the floor, surrounded by a pool of blood, as the mother laid bare on the abortion table, unconscious and unlikely to survive the trauma.

Paranormal Jack Jr. had enough and wanted out, to disconnect from the dark imagery. He felt his hand dragged in farther, but he fought back desperately with his consciousness. The sight of mothers experimented on by a crazy doctor and the presence of dead fetuses beside them made his stomach churn and his guts tighten. His heart pulsated so fast that he could hear his heartbeat pounding in his head, so loud it felt like his head was going to blow up.

Then another image flashed through his mind, accompanied by the giggle of children. It was the laughter of a playground and children swinging off the monkey bars, pushing each other down the slide, and squeaky swings dangling from one side to another. It could have been any playground in a park or next to a school.

He jolted at the sudden appearance of four children of various ages, looking toward him from a distance. The older girl must have been about ten years old and clutched a Teddy bear, while the other children, younger in age, stood next to her. They looked on, emotionless, and without any sense of character, starry-eyed with magnetic blue eyes. They were dressed in clothing like children from the 1800s. They were a living past of sadness, lost and frozen in a transitionary place, not knowing how to find their way out. Caught in a meaningless existence, like a punishment that never ended.

Paranormal Jack Jr. could feel their pain and hurt and a deep sense of wanting to clutch and embrace the comfort of a mother and father. To hold them tight and never let them go.

Then without warning, the vibration stopped, and the children's sensory faded away. It was just him and the mahogany door as he removed his hand from the scratches of the devil's paw.

Paranormal Jack Jr. heard the slow footsteps behind him, thinking Harry was sneaking up intentionally to play a practical joke.

"Is that you, mate, crawling up behind me?" Paranormal Jack Jr. turned then jolted to be faced by an old priest.

"No need to be frightened, my dear boy. It's only me. Sorry for creeping up on you like that." He put out his hand to welcome Paranormal Jack Jr. with a firm handshake.

Paranormal Jack Jr. grimaced, not wanting to embarrass himself from being caught frightened. "Oh, you're Father O'Connor from Saint Peter's, right?"

"Yes, that's me. I thought I'd pass by to see how you're setting up for your paranormal investigation. That's a load of equipment Harry has in his Ute out there."

"Yes Father. It's about getting proof, you know; silence the skeptics. If there's anything in here, that equipment will find it and record it."

Father O'Connor smiled and patted Paranormal Jack Jr. on the back. "Well, if you need any divine intervention, let me know. Although, I always get a sense of dread when I come in here. It was never a happy place, you know." He pointed to the door leading to the basement. "Horrible things happened in that basement."

"Yeah, I got a sense of that when I walked down the stairs to the entrance. Oh, and I couldn't help but notice the scratch marks on the door. Never seen anything like that before."

"Hmm … You are very inquisitive, my son." Father O'Connor paused for a moment and clutched his cross. "Here, take this cross and put it around your neck. It's been blessed by the holy water in my church."

"Oh, thank you, Father … though I'm not the church-going type."

"God will find you, my son. He finds everybody who is willing. And your father, Paranormal Jack Sr. from Hartley Town, God bless his soul. He would have liked you to have this cross."

"You knew my dad?"

"Not personally, but I met him once in Hartley when I visited the town during my vacation. He was a charming and charismatic man and, deep down inside, very spiritual. We chatted for an hour about all sorts of things over tea."

"How coincidental. It's a small world, Father."

"Ah, best be going and let you be. You don't want an old priest hanging around and getting in the way of your investigation."

Father O'Connor squinted and frowned as his cheeks turned red. "Those scratches on the door are the marks of the devil … well, at least that's what the locals say—the devil's paw." He turned and walked toward the entrance just as Harry carried in his first piece of ghostbusting equipment. Father O'Connor nodded to Harry, not saying a word.

"What's the priest doing here?" Harry asked.

"Oh, he was friendly enough, but I think he was snooping around to see what we're up to." Paranormal Jack Jr. helped Harry with the crate as they laid it next to the power cord.

"So, what do you think of the place? Had a look around?"

"Yeah, it's not what I expected for an asylum. They were more progressive back then than I imagined." Paranormal Jack Jr. pointed to the staircase leading to the basement.

"You went to the basement?"

"Yeah, but it's locked. I guess you may have the keys?"

Harry nodded. "Sure. We can check it out when I'm unloaded. You know what they say about basements in haunted buildings?"

Paranormal Jack Jr. grinned. "There's always something down there, right?"

He pointed to the Ute outside, through the main entrance. "You managed to get it up close. That will make unpacking easier. Do you want a hand?"

"No, I'm all right, Jack. Thanks for the offer, but I know where everything is and where to position it in this room."

"Yeah, got it. You're an organized sort of guy. But I do want to tell you something."

"When I get back with my next piece of equipment." Harry gave him the thumbs-up then went back to the Ute to unload more.

Paranormal Jack Jr. was left wondering about his experience at the basement entrance. As so often happened with ghost hunters, they never had anyone to talk to about their encounters, let alone understand it. Harry was a technical guy, into ghostbusting technology, driven by his earlier skeptical views. For him, it was all about finding the evidence. The only person he could discuss the contact with the dark spirit would be Clarisse. But she wasn't coming to Willow Court Asylum until they finished setting up the equipment. For now, he was left pondering his experience at the mahogany door.

Paranormal Jack Jr. felt it was time to explore farther down the hallway of Ward C while Harry unloaded.

The hallways turned in two directions—left and right—and were flanked by more rooms. He had heard a lot about the abortion room and the morgue, so he set out, looking for them.

The abortion room and the morgue featured heavily as the main attraction during the paranormal tours before they had ceased. Mainly because they were well-preserved and because abortions had taken place in the room, with many mothers dying in the process. Back in the 1880s, it had still been a relatively new practice and bound by experimentation.

Something brushed his hip then rattled down the hallway. They were tiny steps but fast, like the sound of a beating drum. He shook his head, unsure what had gripped him, and looked around to find nothing but a chill in the air and an empty expanse.

Then he felt another brush to his other side, clasping his thighs with the slightest of pinches. On this occasion, the running footsteps were not as coordinated. A *thumpity thump* sound of leather shoes on timber floor echoed like the *clip-ity clap* of a tap dancer. In the background was the giggle of two young children having fun.

Was this a game of cat and mouse, playing with him?

The sounds of children didn't have a sinister tone, but it still sent a chill up his spine. It was followed by a morbid silence and unease.

Paranormal Jack Jr. kept walking toward the end of the corridor, unsure whether to turn right or left. It looked the same to him—just another hallway flanked by more rooms.

He turned his head slightly to the left and sighted a little boy in grey shorts and long socks. His mousey-colored, straight hair was parted perfectly to the right, and piercing, electric-blue eyes seemed to penetrate right through him. He had a solemn face, emotionless and expressionless, wanting to say something but unable.

Paranormal Jack Jr. turned his head fully to get a better view, but the little boy was gone, followed by more footsteps and the giggles of children.

It was a simple game—tap, pinch, run, hide, and giggle. Except, they were infant spirits, and hiding between walls and dematerializing into transparent entities only improved the essence of the game. It was making it harder for Jack to locate them, keeping him guessing.

The infant spirits raised the intensity with a bucketful of marbles rolling down the hallway toward Paranormal Jack Jr. He would have to watch his step, or he would lose his footing underneath. But they were not the regular marbles you would find in a school ground, as they followed in a straight line, curling and forming shapes along the way as they dispersed then regrouped again. At first, it resembled a slithering serpent, and then a mouse, followed by a cat.

The giggles of children intensified as they became more engaged by his reaction. A cause and effect were often attributed to the behavior of young children. Were they expecting Paranormal Jack Jr. to enforce his parental prowess and tell them to stop?

As the marbles got closer, he started walking back toward the hallway and main entrance, slowly and steadily at first, while keeping one eye on the marbles and the other on the front entrance.

The infant spirits called out. "Aggies, alley, shooter, taw, bumblebees … Can I have your jaspers?" They were all terms for the different types of marbles.

"Do you want to play? Are you a mibster?" It was the voice of a child no more than seven years old.

Paranormal Jack Jr. was being invited to play a game of marbles, a popular game for young school children during the turn of the century.

"Do you want to play ringers?" another voice called out from the end of the hallway.

He turned around to find the image of another boy, a little older, with a handful of marbles in his hand; yellow and red ones. His icy-blue eyes permeated strongly in the shadow of the dark hallway, as a reminder of the child's unearthly existence.

Ringers was a typical game played in a ten-inch diameter circle. It involved flicking marbles outside the perimeter to score a point. Paranormal Jack Jr. recalled playing with his dad as a child. However, his generation never caught on to the simple game, preferring to play video games instead of outdoor activities as he grew older.

He blinked more than once and pinched his face to make sure he wasn't seeing things, but the child's apparition was still there, holding out his right hand full of different sized marbles toward him.

Paranormal Jack Jr. turned his head gently to the right as he captured a glimpse of daylight in the main hallway entrance. It was twenty or so feet away.

He decided to make a dash for it. He ran as fast as he could as he bolted to the safety of the entrance of Willow Court Asylum. He was puffing and taking in deep breaths, symptomatic of his sudden burst of energy. He was not as fit as he should have been for his age.

His pulse rate and blood pressure had risen significantly from his encounter with the infant spirits. His heart was pounding so hard that he could hear it between his ears, like a drum roll. His throat was dry and stuck from the lack of moisture. He swallowed to regain some mobility with his vocal cords by pushing air from his lungs to clear them.

He wiped the perspiration from his forehead that had formed into tiny droplets that cascaded down his face. His shirt was drenched underneath his armpits as his overheated body showed signs of a survival mechanism kicking in during the uncanny encounter. An adrenaline rush ran through his entire body unknowingly.

As he leaned against the wall, pondering what had just happened, Harry came barging in with more equipment hanging off his shoulders.

"Man, you look like you've seen a ghost. Are you feeling all right, Jack? Have you done a few rounds with a poltergeist?"

Harry dropped his bags on the floor next to the other equipment and glanced toward Paranormal Jack Jr., who had not taken the bait. Usually, he would come back with a reply just as good. Still, Paranormal Jack Jr. looked shell-shocked from his experience, gazing directly down the hallway, fixated on whether a ghost would reappear at any moment.

Harry walked up to him and tapped him on the shoulder. "Snap out of it, Jack. You saw something, didn't you?"

Paranormal Jack Jr. nodded and continued staring

down the hallway.

"The spirit box; do you have it with you?"

Paranormal Jack Jr. nodded again then placed his hand in his side pocket to retrieve it. Unknowingly, during his encounter with the infant spirits, he had recorded the vibrations from the spirit world.

"That's good Jack, because if you came across something, it would have recorded the spirit voices."

Harry took a bottle of water from his backpack and handed it to Paranormal Jack Jr. "Here, you look dehydrated and sweaty. But don't ask me how; there's a chill in the air."

He thrust the spirit device in front of Harry and said, "Here, see if there's anything recorded."

Harry took the device and pressed the playback. Then they tentatively waited for the voices of the dark spirits. However, the initial voices were muddled and fuzzy, like static and interference—incongruent and unable to decipher.

"Are you sure this device is working?" Jack asked.

"Just give it a few moments to adjust the vibrations. It's scrambling to recognize the sound and fine-tune the frequency—a new feature I developed to translate unheard vibrations."

The static changed to a coarse sound, like the deep

throat force of a demon's lungs. However, the sound was also underpinned by the voices of young children in the background.

"*Come play with me.*" It was the voice of the older girl.

"*Do you want to play marbles?*" came from a younger boy.

Then all four of the infant spirits spoke simultaneously, a clatter of voices and giggles, making it challenging to decipher.

It was what the demon wanted them to hear as a false sense of security. Who wouldn't be put off by the gentle voices of children wanting to play? And, even though the sounds of the demon were not recognizable, playing out in a different vibration or tongue, it was spine-tingling. What were they dealing with?

"I think that's enough." Harry switched off the spirit box.

Paranormal Jack Jr. frowned and squinted, unsure what to make of the recording. "Is there anyone who can decipher that demonic voice?"

Harry shrugged. "You're asking the wrong person. It's out of my league, Jack. I'm the technical guy when it comes to this stuff."

"Well, you won't believe what I saw when you were gathering the equipment."

"What?"

"It was the most confronting experience of children asking me to play with them."

"Huh?"

"Two boys and two girls. The oldest would have been around twelve years old. They all had these bright-blue, piercing eyes, almost hypnotic, and white faces." Paranormal Jack Jr. crossed his arms and stared him in the eye. "You probably think I'm nuts, don't you?"

"Hey, Jack." Harry patted him on the back. "If I told you stories of what Clarisse and I have seen in other towns, the hairs on your back would stand up."

"And that basement down the stairs ..."

"Yes, I know. Something bad happened in there," Harry interrupted.

"So, what do we do now?"

"Help me power up this stuff. I will set the cameras on night vision and delayed time recording while we go back and get Clarisse."

Harry unzipped the bag that contained his prized piece of equipment—the thermal night vision. "The thermal scopes perform a lot better when it comes to extremely dark settings," he said.

Harry was expecting to capture the movements of the spirit entities based on his previous experience. Since these devices relied on heat instead of light, there was better rendering potential. He expected to capture the movement of spirits at Willow Court Asylum in places his infrared camera had failed in the past.

"Jack, whatever you encountered today, my cameras will find them. And if there are infant spirits in this building, I will get the evidence we need once and for all."

"And if we find evidence of the spirits, then what?"

"Well Jack, that's for you and Clarisse to work out; help them transition to the other side, unlock their curse."

"And what about the demon who's occupied this building for over a hundred and fifty years?"

Harry didn't respond right away. Although he was previously a skeptic and now believed in ghosts, the demon world was not something he had come to terms with yet. He was accepting of their existence, but he was not convinced. The evidence he had obtained of demons during past encounters had been insufficient and needed validation. Spirituality didn't provide all the answers for him, either. Deep down he was still looking for unequivocal evidence of demons, though he wasn't prepared to admit it.

7 THE BASEMENT OF MISERY

"How did it go with setting up the equipment?" Clarisse asked.

He gave her the thumbs-up. "All set and ready to go when you are."

"And what about Jack?"

"Licking his wounds, I guess. He looked rattled and said he saw things."

"What type of things?"

"You know, the usual stuff—ghosts and the sounds of children." Harry shrugged, not wanting to make a big deal of it.

"Anything else that comes to mind?" Harry always had to be pressed for more detail.

"Well, he kept talking about a basement and felt drawn to it, but he couldn't get in." Harry took the keys out of his pocket. "I'm sure one of these will open it."

"Hmm …" She put her hands on her hips, stared at him with a bold look, and waited.

"There's an ornate staircase next to the entrance that leads to the basement—you can't miss it, Clarisse." Harry took the spirit box from his side pocket and lifted it toward her. "To his credit, we did capture voices, so he's telling the truth."

"So, he did experience a paranormal event?"

Harry winked while he played the spirit box recording back to her. It was the same interference and static followed by the voices of little children playing in the background.

"*Come play with me …*" It was the voice of an older girl, of around twelve years of age.

"*Do you want to play marbles?*" a younger boy asked.

Then all four of the infant spirits spoke simultaneously as a clatter of voices and giggles, making it challenging to decipher what was being said.

Clarisse nodded in acknowledgment. "It's the everyday sounds of children having fun at a playground." Clarisse looked down and paused for a moment while she placed her hands together under her chin.

"Oh, and how could I forget? Father O'Connor made an impromptu visit. He's got a habit of appearing out of nowhere," Harry said.

"Out of thin air?" Clarisse interrupted.

"Yeah."

"There's a reason for that."

"What do you mean? He's got a connection with Willow Court?"

"No, nothing sinister. I mean to say, the church is connected. It goes back hundreds of years, and I think he knows more than what he lets on."

She took hold of Harry's arm. "Let's get Jack and make our way to Willow Court. I'm keen to find out what's going on in that place."

"He did make one interesting comment."

"And ...?"

"There were scratches on the door to the basement ..."

Clarisse narrowed her eyes, waiting for him to continue.

"He said the scratches were marks of the devil, and that evil things happened in that room."

"Did he elaborate?"

Harry shrugged. "Hmm ... It's not the first or last time we'll encounter that tight-lipped mentality. Remember Hartley and Old Tailem Town? It was like extracting teeth to get them to share their knowledge."

Clarisse nodded. "How could I forget? I was so frustrated with the locals that I felt like kicking them sometimes." Clarisse paused momentarily and closed her eyes while taking a deep breath.

"What is it, Clarisse?"

"I read about the abortion chair at Willow Court while you were setting up with Jack. There was another abortion room ... a secret one where more horrific events happened."

Harry sensed what she was getting at. "But my research tells me it's not in the basement; it's a separate room in Ward C. We can check it out when we get there. Apparently, when they were running the ghost tours out of Willow Court, it was the main attraction." Harry paused then asked, "You've sensed it?"

Clarisse nodded as the pain of the room ripped through her body. A tear formed in her tear duct, and her face mellowed with sadness.

Harry knew she felt something sinister, and her extrasensory had latched on to dark, spiritual energy.

"You can feel the vibration from here, Clarisse?"

"Evil has no boundaries, and it will come looking for you. Especially if it knows it can connect with me."

"Evil speaks to you?"

"Evil comes looking for me. It tries to incite fear; a warning sign so I will go away. It's a dark spirit, and whatever's in that basement is sinister."

"Well, I don't think you'll be going alone into the

basement while you're pregnant. Maybe Jack and I can do the initial inspection. I have video cam technology that can link to your phone, so you can watch us explore the room live."

"Like a documentary?"

"I promise I won't talk too much and provide commentary."

Clarisse smiled and tugged on Harry's arm. "Let's go get Jack."

Upon their arrival at Willow Court Asylum, Clarisse felt uneasy. Flashbacks of voices of children playing in the playground and calling out for her to join them repeated in her mind. She shook her head to dispel the thoughts, but they were a powerful insight of what to expect.

Paranormal Jack Jr. kicked open the temporary gate with his right leg, thrusting it forward. It ricocheted off the top fence post and bounced around. It had been flimsily put together and was useless at keeping out the squatters and vagabonds.

Harry watched on with a frown. "Didn't you lock the gate on the way out, Jack?"

"Yeah, I did. Maybe I didn't do a good job of it. The padlock must be fifty years old, rusted. I'm surprised it still works."

"They spent all this money on useless fencing and couldn't afford a decent lock?" Harry turned his head from side to side. He was always the type who believed equipment should be up to date and in good working order.

Clarisse followed suit as they walked up the steps of Willow Court and onto the squeaky, timber floor that was lifting in parts due to lack of repair. Some of them had rusty, protruding nail heads that they walked around to the main entrance.

"It's sad how they've left this place rot. A historic building, over one hundred and fifty years old," Clarisse stated.

"I don't think the locals care," Harry replied. "It's a symbol of angst for them—bad memories. I haven't heard anyone say anything good about this building."

"So, why do you think they want a paranormal investigation? Why bother and waste the money?" Clarisse raised a good point.

"Hmm ... Well, if I put my business hat on, it may have to do with convincing the locals that all the myths and superstitions are just folklore. Get them to mentally move on and introduce tourism to the town. Run tours of Willow Court Asylum and the barracks surrounding it. Sell it as a piece of Australian history. And when you think about it, New Norfolk has some of the oldest buildings in this country. It was settled in 1807; the third oldest colony in Tasmania."

"You're a wealth of knowledge, Harry," Paranormal Jack Jr. called out as he waved to them from inside the asylum, "but I think there's something you will want to see inside." He pointed to the equipment that Harry had set up before they had left. Everything had fallen to the side from their support stands, as though pushed over deliberately.

"What happened here?" Harry was unhappy that his equipment had been tampered with.

"It may explain why the padlock was open—someone broke in, maybe?"

Harry quickly stepped over to the equipment to assess if there was any damage. "It doesn't look broken, just fallen to the side, thank God. Maybe a strong breeze?"

"Or someone pushed them over?" Clarisse called out. "There are lots of people in town who are unhappy about us being here."

"The red light's still on the night vision camera, and it hasn't stopped recording." Harry gently lifted the camera back onto the tripod. Then he nodded toward Clarisse and Jack Jr., who were only a couple of feet away. "Let's see what we've got here."

Harry played back the recording and waved to Clarisse and Paranormal Jack Jr. "Well, come on; get closer so we can all watch."

They huddled around as they viewed the nine-inch monitor, eagerly waiting for the images from the recording.

"It's Father O'Connor," Clarisse said.

"He came back after we left to pick you up." Harry zoomed in. "He's got keys in his right hand."

"And a wooden cross in the other hand," Paranormal Jack Jr. interrupted.

"And he looks determined. Notice he keeps looking toward the stairs leading to the basement." Harry pointed to the stairs directly in front of them that occupied the main entrance to Willow Court Asylum.

"Harry, he's not fiddling with the camera equipment. Something else pushed them over," Clarisse said.

Paranormal Jack Jr. scratched his head. "There's something down there in the basement, and it's not friendly."

The camera recording was in night vision mode, moving away from Father O'Connor to an ominous energy source directly in front of him.

"See that outline? It's shaped like—"

"A demon," Clarisse interjected. "Look at its outline and configuration—devil horns and the body of a half-man, half-animal."

"It's walking on hooves like a wildebeest." Paranormal Jack Jr.'s voice had lifted a decibel.

Father O'Connor wasn't startled by the terror in front of him. He came prepared to confront it, but why?

They watched the recording as he lifted his cross toward the demonic figure outwardly while on his knees. Father O'Connor then placed the cross on the floor and took a bottle of holy water from his pocket. He sprinkled the holy water in a circle around him, creating an area of protection from the approaching demon. Then he retrieved his pocket-sized Holy Bible, read out scriptures in a persuasive manner, and raised his hands toward the sky.

"He's confronting the demon with scriptures and holy prayer," Clarisse commented.

"He knows more about the evil that lurks in this place than we thought," Paranormal Jack Jr. said. "Do you have audio, Harry?"

"Yeah, but it's muzzled by a kinetic type of energy, and it's drowning out the sound." He adjusted the volume and the recording sound to clear the interference. Still, all he could achieve was crackling static sound.

"I've never seen a dark energy that can drown out sounds and interfere with the equipment before." Clarisse frowned and creased her eyes while clutching her hands.

Harry nodded. "Yeah, we've always been able to decipher the sound somehow. I remember, in Hartley, we had the same problem, but we isolated the voices on the recording."

Father O'Connor continued praying with vigor as he held the pocketbook Bible in his right hand. With a staunchly determined expression, he clenched his fist and accentuated the creases around his face. His forceful demeanor was not built on anger but by the spirit inside him. It wasn't a physical battle as such, but his belief in God was his weapon.

In the camera recording, they saw the image of a demon moving toward him. It would retreat when confronted by the pure energy that Father O'Connor embodied in the circle. Then the demon lifted its arms and screeched in anger, blowing all the equipment onto the floor from their tripod stand. The fall didn't stop the camera recording on an angle; this time, coincidentally, toward the stairs leading to the basement.

"Oh my God!" Clarisse exclaimed.

"Are those the entities you confronted while I was unloading the Ute?" Harry turned immediately to Paranormal Jack Jr.

"Yes, they are the ghosts I saw. That little boy is the kid with the marbles."

Standing on the steps of the staircase were four children—two girls and two boys, dressed in eighteenth-century clothing. They watched on, giggling innocently as their icy-blue eyes penetrated the camera lens with a haze effect. They were watching the master demon at play, like a sideshow, as it ventured toward Father O'Connor.

The oldest of the children was a girl of at least twelve years of age. She held a Teddy bear, hugging it next to her face. The youngest child flicked marbles into the air and caught them before they reached the ground. The other two children had their hands on their hips and looked on without making any movements. They were comfortable watching the demon at play.

Father O'Connor was an old man, and there was only so much energy he could exert in a dust-up with the powerful demon. And, like many times before, he had done enough to remind the evil entity of his ability.

He stood up and placed the pocket Bible in his pocket. And, while holding the cross in his right hand, he retreated to the entrance while splashing holy water in front of him to create a barrier. The skirmish was over quickly. The recording had lasted under five minutes.

"Hmm … It was a run-in with the demon that didn't last very long," Harry said.

Clarisse tapped him on the shoulder and responded,

"He was trying to protect us."

Paranormal Jack Jr. had a perplexed look on his face. "I don't get it. What was his encounter supposed to do with us?"

Clarisse was looking smug as she folded her arms across her chest. "You don't think that demon knows we're here? You think it doesn't see us as a threat, Jack?"

He nodded in agreement. "Well, it makes sense when you put it that way. It may explain the children trying to contact me, also."

"Yep, trying to ward us off and using the infant spirits as a decoy; testing our resolve." Clarisse closed her eyes and held her hands together, deep in thought, attempting to connect with the spirits in the house.

Paranormal Jack Jr. wanted to say something, but Harry put his fingers across his lips. "Not now, Jack. She's trying to connect with the spirits."

Clarisse became expressionless and apathetic to anything around her. She was entering a different spirit world as her mind raced off. Harry had seen this before during her connections at Old Tailem Town. It was a skill she had learned from Shamy, the local shaman and religious recluse.

If she focused hard enough and allowed her mind to wander, she could feel the energy field around her and see images of dead people. And, when things got messy, she could also see how they died, particularly under mysterious circumstances. Shamy had taught her to respond to the pain by maintaining an awareness of where she was. That way, she could disconnect and come back to the real time. There was always a danger that, if she stayed in their spiritual dimension for too long, they could pull her away.

Clarisse closed her eyes, but there was the movement of her pupils pressing on her eyelids. She was in a meditated state with her hands clutched together and her fingers wiggling intermittently. She was transposed to a moment that would become every mother's harrowing nightmare— the loss of a child.

Harry waved to Paranormal Jack Jr. "Don't touch her, Jack. She's tapped into something."

"She's in a trance-like state."

"Connecting with the spirit world; a throwback usually about an event that happened in the past."

Jack folded his arms across his chest. "Is it dangerous stepping into the unknown?"

Harry took a deep breath. "She's done it before, many times, and had the best teacher in Old Tailem Town. It was the shaman who taught her to refine her technique."

Clarisse was transposed to Willow Court Asylum, 1889,

inside Abbey's room. In fact, it was across the hallway in Ward C from where Clarisse, Harry, and Paranormal Jack Jr. were currently standing.

Abbey lay in her bed as the rays of the early morning sun filtered through the ripped curtains. Speckles of dust particles captured by the yellowish rays of light beamed inside and danced in the air. She enjoyed watching nature's display on sunny days. It was her only relief to ponder about what could have been and imagine; otherwise, it was a plain, dreary room. And this was despite the attempts of the doctor to brighten up the place with limestone colors to create a livelier ambiance.

But that was not the only event that captured Abbey's attention. Something more sinister had presented itself at her door.

Her stomach churned, and her guts curdled inside out from the pain. Knowing her time had come to give up the soul of her child, she was in a state of flux, powerless to negotiate or change the course of events.

The demon leaned against the door and crossed his legs casually. It was not perturbed by the quest to fetch the child. After all, the arrangement had been sealed ten years ago.

"You can't have my child!" Abbey pointed to the demon standing by the door. She had an aggressive look on her face, like any mother protecting their child.

"Oh Abbey, how people forget their arrangements so conveniently. It's time to take him away. We agreed when I saved you, too, when maybe I shouldn't have. But I went beyond the call of duty and saved mother and son. I have never done that before and was scolded by my superiors for acting too much like an angel. I was told to toughen up. So there will be no deals today, despite your protestations."

Abbey didn't remember agreeing because she hadn't. Dr. Monserrat had made the deal for her. However, because she would have made the deal, she believed the demon.

"I'll do anything to keep him. Name your price, demon. Why don't you take me instead? I will trade my life for his. Take me." She was on the edge of tears, and the only thing holding her together was her need to change the demon's mind.

"Oh, and how I admire your strength of sacrifice for your child. It's very Christian of you; I can see that. But I have no need for you. It would be a futile arrangement. It's the child I want, and it's time, as per our arrangement ten years ago." The demon crossed his arms and tapped his feet impatiently. "I saved him from certain death, haven't you forgotten? You've had ten good years with him, uninterrupted, and now he's mine to do what I wish." The demon stood firm and winked at her sarcastically. It enjoyed the pain of watching a mother let go of their child against their will.

Abbey broke down in tears and sobbed. "Name your price, demon. Anything. Take my soul instead. Take it now!"

The demon shrugged and didn't respond, having made itself clear—the child's soul would become his, and so he needn't do anything. It would happen irrespective of whether another deal with the devil was made. Their previous arrangement would stand with no turning back.

"Will I ever see him again?" Abbey called out as she rolled over in her bed and gripped her belly. It was a mother's pain so intense it absorbed her whole body as tension ripped through her.

"No, my dear. Never again. But the news isn't good for you, either."

"What do you mean?"

"You'll also die from wounds sustained ten years ago during childbirth. A recurrence of your injury because your doctor didn't patch you up properly at the time. It will happen tonight in your sleep, as you bleed internally. I've decided to make it as painless as possible. The doctors won't stop the bleeding, as they can't perform that procedure in this century. You were supposed to die anyway while the boy lived, but I had a moment of charity and allowed you to stay by his side until it was his time."

The demon paused and thought about its following words. "Maybe letting you live was a mistake that I had to endure with my masters, but nobody's perfect. I won't be doing that again. Next time, I will let the mother die. Less cumbersome later."

The demon pondered his thoughts for a moment. "Your boy could have been the fifth child. It would have closed off the curse. But you were not the right candidate. The fifth child must be a newborn and come from a mother who has tenacity and spiritual prowess—a strong belief in your God and a spirit hunter. Now *that's* a worthy catch."

Abbey was furious as she picked up an empty glass and threw it toward the demon. "You monster! You tricked me." It smashed into the wall then broke into fragments of broken glass, splattering onto the floor across the entrance to her room.

"My dear, has anyone told you not to trust a demon?" The demon turned its back on her then disappeared through the thin walls. And, while doing so, the echo of its voice filled the room. "It was discussed with you, but you were in so much pain at the time you agreed to everything I asked. But don't take it out on yourself; ninety-nine percent of mothers would have done the same."

Abbey felt a gripping, sharp pain as she clasped her belly once more and called out for the duty nurse. "Help me! Someone help me." Blood trickled onto the white sheets.

"But I have one proposition for you." The devil was not visible in the room, but its voice filled the air, nevertheless. "So, hear me out, my dear ... while you suffer in pain." The demon paused for a moment. "When you die, I will let you be with your boy in the spirit world. And I'm not talking about heaven. It's my spirit world, under my control and my rules, a place between death and immortality; a transient place that I've created for the infant spirits."

"I get to be with him when I die? All the time?"

"Yes. All the time and without any restrictions. Heck, you can look after the other children, too, while I tend to other things. Be their nanny, so to speak. Who said that death was bad after all?"

"You want me to look after the souls of other infants while I'm dead?"

"Yes, if you want to be with your child. A small price to pay for the love of your boy, don't you think?"

"Do I have your word, demon? How can I trust you?" Abbey asked.

"I'm a demon; you can't trust me ... But, if you want a

contract with the devil in writing, that can be arranged. Written contracts with demons must be honored, like scriptures. My masters wouldn't like it if I reneged on a devil's contract."

Abbey realized she had been thrown a lifeline by the demon and only because he needed someone to look over the infant spirits. Or maybe it had let her live ten years ago because it had anticipated the need.

She was gorgeous and a sight to behold. Even a demon could see the value of keeping her around and gracing its underworld with her good looks. Plus, his flock of infant spirits was growing up, and he underestimated the effort required to show them his evil ways, nurturing them in the name of the devil.

But deep inside, all Abbey could see in front of her was living in a mental institution. No matter how much social engineering the doctors attempted to reform the patient treatment, she would always be a mental patient, shunned by her wealthy family. The alternative of being dead and living amongst the souls of infant spirits and her son was better than her current life. It made her choice easier, one that didn't require too much agonizing. In Abbey's case, being dead carried some benefits. She would free herself from the anguish of being locked away in a mental institution for the rest of her life.

Clarisse snapped back to the real world to find Harry and Paranormal Jack Jr. standing in front of her. Her watery eyes and the disturbed look on her face worried them.

"It wasn't good?" Harry, who could sense her reaction to flashbacks, asked.

She wiped her eyes and cleared her throat as she regained consciousness in the present time. "You don't want to know what went on in this place."

"Tell us; we need to know what we're dealing with," Paranormal Jack Jr. demanded.

She paused and thought about what she had witnessed in her flashback. "The infant spirits are controlled by a demon that has created a network of children to perform its nasty deeds. And there's a woman … Her name is Abbey, the mother of a ten-year-old boy. She made a pact with the demon that when she died, she would become their nanny in the afterlife."

"But she hasn't shown herself in any of my encounters."

"Jack, not everything happens all at once with dark spirits. I'm sure she'll show herself when the time is right."

Clarisse crinkled her forehead and closed her eyes while clasping her hands. "I saw something else that I wasn't supposed to." Clarisse was reluctant to say more.

"Tell us, Clarisse. Try hard." Harry rubbed her shoulder

then placed his hands gently on her face while tears rolled down, trickling onto his hands.

"It was the most horrible thing I've ever seen, Harry." She paused.

"Look into my eyes, Clarisse. We need to know what you saw."

"It was an abortion room … blood everywhere, mothers screaming, and …"

"And what?"

"Dead fetuses on the floor. Some were in large jars from previous experiments. It was a chamber of horrors. Experiments went on this room … the cruelest type by a madman." She pointed to the staircase that led to the basement.

"Is that where the experiments took place?" Harry asked.

Clarisse nodded and found it difficult to express herself. "Evil lurks in that room and the dead souls of babies. A slaughterhouse of inconceivable acts of torture at the hands of the head doctor at the time." Clarisse paused to gather her thoughts. "His name was Dr. Pendergrass."

8 DR. MONSERRAT'S DIARY

Night had settled on New Norfolk, and Ward C took on a different ambiance. The battery-powered lamps, which were their only source of light, extended ten feet around them. Beyond that perimeter, it was pitch black. Like any other creepy building of its time, Ward C had a character of its own—uninviting, nippy, and lifeless.

"I read a passage in Dr. Monserrat's diary that commented about physical objects holding paranormal energy sources," Harry said. They sat on picnic chairs around the ghostbusting equipment, waiting for something to trigger the devices. The waiting game.

Clarisse took an interest in the discussion as it reminded her of her family home and the scarlet chair. It had been passed down for generations and had possessed an evil energy source. "An object can't hold the spirit of someone who has passed away, even though they may not have moved on to the other side. However, an object can keep that person's energy for a long time, if that energy can be fed and nurtured with superstition. The power can be positive, negative, or in-between, or evolve into something more sinister," she said.

Harry nodded in acknowledgment. "How could I forget my first encounter with the spirit world and the scarlet chair?" He took a sip of his tea then placed the cup in front of him. "But this time, it's not as simple as an antique chair in a family home. Dr. Monserrat refers to the sinister powers in an abortion chair." Harry cleared his throat gently. "In his notes, he states that the abortion room is evil."

"Apparently, it's one of the few rooms that haven't been vandalized by squatters," Paranormal Jack Jr. interrupted.

"Who would want to sleep in an abortion room?" Harry was trying to make a point.

"What else did Dr. Monserrat's diary mention of importance?" Clarisse asked.

"Hmm ... I remember reading the abortion chair is attached to an old spirit. Her name is Abbey, verified by three psychic mediums at the time, and you now," Harry answered, impressing her with his research.

"Hmm ... So, Abbey's spirit has attached to the

abortion chair. Anything else?"

Harry paused while he collected his thoughts. "Oh yes, you'll like this one. The morgue next to the abortion room is haunted. Apparently, it gets very nasty."

"How convenient. Does anyone know where it's located?"

"According to the old drawing we got from Gary, it's farther down the hallway, to the left side of the ward, right down the back of the building." Harry had a copy of the layout of Ward C in his backpack and reached for it. He unfolded and laid it on the floor while shining his flashlight to read the diagram. "We're here, and the abortion room is there, next to the morgue." He pointed to the spot on the drawing with his index finger as Clarisse and Paranormal Jack Jr. moved in closer to get a look.

"Yes, it's over there to the left." Clarisse lifted her hand into the empty, pitch-black darkness of Ward C.

"Let's go and check it now," Jack said in an impromptu manner. "Or are we going to sit here all night and talk about Dr. Monserrat's diary?"

Clarisse looked at Harry and shrugged. "I'm up for it Jack, if you want to lead the way?"

"Are you sure, Clarisse? You don't want to wait until sunrise?" Harry had been spooked by Dr. Monserrat's notes.

"You look worried, Harry. That's not like you. Is there something else you want to say?" Clarisse asked, her big brown eyes penetrating him as she often did when pressing for information.

"Well, this has nothing to do with Dr. Monserrat's diary. There was an incident last year during a paranormal tour …" He took a deep breath then sighed.

"Come on, mate; out with it. Tell us what happened," Paranormal Jack Jr. urged.

"A teenage girl, who was fooling around during the ghost tour, sat down on the abortion chair as part of a do-or-dare. And despite being told not to, she snuck in there when they left the room to visit the morgue."

"And …?" Clarisse was impatient.

"She was found by her mother, unconscious, and with marks all over her wrists and ankles."

"As though she'd been tied to the chair?" Clarisse asked.

"Yeah, and when she finally woke up, she was hysterical, clutching her belly. It took her an hour to calm down."

"Did they find out what happened to her? Did she provide an explanation?"

"No, she never spoke about it until one day she agreed to have hypnotherapy to learn what had happened to her." Harry held his hands together and looked toward both Clarisse and Paranormal Jack Jr. "Is that enough detail now?"

"You're not going to tell us what happened next?" Paranormal Jack Jr. pressed.

"Huh, if you thought the scarlet chair was bad, and if you recall, it could tap into your mind and gather your most fearful thoughts if you sat on it—"

"The abortion chair does the same?" Clarisse interrupted.

Harry didn't respond as he pointed his flashlight toward the end of the hallway. "Are you both ready to visit the morgue and the abortion room? It's what we agreed to do, right?"

"Harry, I want to know. I can handle it. Seriously, I've been through worse at Hartley and Old Tailem Town." She grabbed his arm and tugged. "Trust me, Harry." She stared him into submission with her brazen look. Clarisse had a knack for getting what she wanted from Harry, if she pulled the right levers.

Paranormal Jack Jr. looked on and didn't say a word. He knew it was between Harry and Clarisse.

"The girl experienced the abortion of a child that was two months premature. She screamed in pain as the mad doctor experimented with high forceps techniques to maneuver the child. He was using her as an experiment with new tools and techniques. To see her threshold for pain and how far the body could take it before the child would die."

"He deliberately killed the child in the process." Clarisse took a step back and placed her hands over her face.

"I warned you, Clarisse." Harry was incensed that she hadn't heeded his advice.

"And the baby? What happened to it?" Clarisse asked.

"It died during the procedure, like all the babies; sacrificed for a rogue doctor's experiments. Blood covered the table and spilled on the floor while the dead baby was extracted at the last minute to save the woman before she bled to death."

"He nearly killed the mother, too?"

"She was the lucky one. Many women died during his experiments. Each time he failed to perfect his technique, he discarded the baby onto the floor and called in another woman."

"Where did you get this detail, Harry?" Paranormal Jack Jr. gulped as his throat tightened up.

"I got it from Dr. Monserrat's journal. The mad doctor was eventually expelled and taken to prison for malpractice and murder, but it was all hushed up after that. Those responsible for overseeing Willow Court Asylum didn't want to expose the cruel acts and cause controversy."

"Do you think the locals know about this story?"

Clarisse asked.

"That, I don't know. But I can say that Dr. Monserrat's diaries aren't a secret and can be obtained freely from the national archives."

"Is that how you got hold of the information?"

"Yes."

"But how did you know who to look for?" Paranormal Jack Jr. was curious and raised his eyebrows.

"Oh, don't you worry. Harry knows how to research and finds things you would never imagine," Clarisse told him wide-eyed.

"Huh, you're a real paranormal sleuth."

Harry nodded then threw his hands up in the air. "Can we visit the morgue and the abortion room now, as we agreed? Why don't you lead the way, Jack? It's at the end of the hallway, and then we turn left and proceed to the back of the building."

Paranormal Jack Jr. obliged, not saying a word, knowing he had pushed Harry enough for one day

He led the way through the empty corridors, with Clarisse and Harry following behind. As they passed by each door, they realized it was a timestamp of history. A mentally ill patient lived here for most of their life; some with conditions that today would have been treated with prescribed medicine and counseling. They had not been the misfits or derelicts that their families had portrayed them to be. But social standing had been fickle back then. How could a wealthy family not represent itself as perfect in the eyes of others?

As they got closer to the end of the hallway, they heard children jumping rope and giggling. They stopped and looked at each other, perplexed as to where the sound was coming from—it appeared to be all around them. They were singing and having fun. A playful ambiance filled the air.

> *"Johnny broke a bottle and blamed it on me.*
> *I told ma, ma told pa.*
> *Johnny got a spanking, so ha-ha-ha.*
> *How many spankings did Johnny get?*
> *1, 2, 3 ... "*

"Did you hear that?" Clarisse asked. They were singing "Down by the River."

"I never played jumping rope games when I was growing up, so I wouldn't know," Harry said.

Paranormal Jack Jr. nodded then shrugged. "I was too busy playing on Dad's farm with the animals." He flashed his flashlight three hundred and sixty degrees but couldn't see anything despite the rhythmic tunes continuing.

"Teddy bear, Teddy bear, touch the ground.
Teddy bear, Teddy bear, show your shoe.
Teddy bear, Teddy bear, that will do!
Teddy bear, Teddy bear, go upstairs.
Teddy bear, Teddy bear, say your prayers.
Teddy bear, Teddy bear, turn out the lights.
Teddy bear, Teddy bear, say goodnight!"

They heard voices of children and their footsteps tapping on the floor as they joined the jumping rope game, each child taking turns. Every time a rhyme ended, another child took their turn to hold the rope. The skipping rope hit the timber floor with a clapping sound, creating a uniformity, like a beating drum. The dark void of Ward C had transformed into lively excelsior of fun-loving children.

But it was the moot point, and Clarisse understood this more than anyone else. The infant spirits were the front line of the demon who had occupied Willow Court for over a century. They were used as a decoy to confuse paranormal investigators into thinking the sweetness and innocence of young infant spirits graced the building. And how on earth could an innocent child hurt you?

As they turned down the hallway leading directly to the old morgue and the abortion room, the sound of the children ceased. There was only darkness, a chill in the air, and dead silence, as though nothing had ever happened.

As Harry turned to get a glimpse of the children, he was pelted by marbles that came out of nowhere. It was followed by the giggles of a boy.

"I felt something brush me and pinch my leg," he said.

More marbles came rolling down the hallway toward them—aggies, immies, cat's eyes, and alleys in their multitude of vibrant colors. They reflected off the flashlight like a glittering prize. At least fifty in different sizes as the grinding sound of rolling glass on timber filled the room. A trail of standard and large marbles all mixed and reverberated as the sound intensified like a hundred footsteps stomping on the floor.

Harry took hold of Clarisse's arm and pulled her to the side as Paranormal Jack Jr. jumped out of the way. But rather than being overawed by it all, he took it in stride with a childish smirk. If Willow Court wasn't such a spooky place and uninviting, one would think he was enjoying the moment.

They reached the abortion room and hastily made their way inside, away from the playful acts of the infant spirits. Then the door to the abortion room shut behind them with a thumping *bang*. The room was dark and only a twinkle of light penetrated through the cracks between the door and the floor.

Paranormal Jack Jr. adjusted his flashlight as it flickered on and off without a reason. He knew from discussions with his father that some energies could interfere with equipment. It was a problem because he never knew if a blackout would occur during his ghost tours, leaving the tourists gasping for air amid the dark shades of night.

"I can't get the damn torch to light up," he said in frustration.

"Mine's not working at all, either," Harry said as he tapped on his several times.

Then the sound of a little girl singing "Hide and Seek" filled the room in an impromptu manner. It was a raspy shrill that sang in tune without missing a beat. And, though it had the innocence of a child going about its playful chant, it was underpinned by a sinister rendition. The voice giggled mischievously in-between phrases as it echoed throughout the room in a monotone pitch

> *"Hide and seek. Hide and seek.*
> *Let's play hide and seek.*
> *Hide and seek. Hide and seek.*
> *Let's play hide and seek."*

The voice changed to a little boy humming a lullaby

without singing the words. It was a younger voice, harmless and so angelic you wanted to hold him in your arms like a Teddy bear. It was an unassuming rendition that could have come from a professional boys' choir. They had never heard such purity in sound, to the point it made them want to capture the moment and stop time, just for a moment.

> "*La, la, la,*
> *La, la, la.*
> *La, la, la, la, la, la, la.*
> *la, la, la.*
> *La, la, la.*"

In the background, his voice was backed up by the sound of plucking bell tones vibrating throughout the room like a music box. And, once more, the sounds of children's giggling overlaid the music box and the humming repertoire of the boy's voice. The experience was misleading and enough to make you feel comfortable, that it wasn't so bad at Willow Court Asylum. But Clarisse knew the tricks of the demon—to provide you with a false sense of security.

There was a chill in the air as Clarisse buttoned up her jacket and blew on her hands to warm them up.

Paranormal Jack Jr. managed to get the flashlight

working again and immediately flashed it around the room. He was startled by the incandescent image of a woman—an orange, yellow outline that glistened and shimmered erratically.

Her long, black hair partially covered her face, although it was difficult to see much beyond the counters of her shadow. Was it the minder overlooking the infant spirits?

The spirit breathed heavily, with long, deep sounds, as it struggled to exhale from its lungs.

"Is it you, Abbey? We know about what happened with your child and the pact you made with the devil," Clarisse said, unperturbed by the ghastly image.

Abbey raised her right hand and pointed to Clarisse's belly with her index finger. She was trying to say something but couldn't speak. Abbey then pointed to the abortion chair, as though she meant to convey a message.

Clarisse placed her hands on her belly and felt the uncontrollable kicks of her six-month-old child, reacting to the evil energy sources in the room.

Harry watched on, concerned and with one thought only. "We need to get you out of here, Clarisse!" He grabbed her arm and began pulling her away from Abbey's spirit.

"It's not pointing at her stomach; it's pointing toward the abortion chair," Paranormal Jack Jr. said.

"Little boy, little boy,
Go to sleep now, little boy.
And in your dreams,
You'll see,
All your toys that you love to please."

The room filled with the sound of Abbey singing to her child, and then a younger boy's image appeared simultaneously next to Abbey's ghost. The boy was ten years old, wearing a white shirt and a sleeveless pullover. His straight, brown hair was parted to one side, with a short back and sides. His long, grey socks were pushed up to his knees, almost joining his knee-length brown shorts. The boy was expressionless, with one hand in his pocket, standing motionless as he held Abbey's hand. Was it her son?

Paranormal Jack Jr. continued shining the flashlight on the energy source surrounding Abbey—an aura of glowing light blue that filled the void she occupied. He walked backward by taking short steps toward the entrance of the room and grabbed hold of the doorknob, turning it enough until he heard the clicking sound of the lock disengaging.

Harry and Clarisse followed tentatively as the room continued to fill with children singing like a choir.

In the background were the backup vocals of a brutally distorted manipulation—the cries of death of the mothers who hadn't survived the doctor's experiments. Moaning and agonizing murmurs of women in the early throes of bleeding to death. Helpless and desperate to stay alive at all costs. It was their final attempt to cling to life, already scarred by the loss of their child.

Paranormal Jack Jr. flung the door open and waved to Clarisse and Harry to leave the room quickly. Clarisse exited first before slipping over a trail of marbles deliberately left laying on the floor. She lost her balance, falling onto her back.

"Ouch!" she shrieked, clasping her lower back.

Harry rushed to her aid, immediately concerned the fall might have hurt the child. Paranormal Jack Jr dashed toward Clarisse and took hold of her shoulder. Harry supported Clarisse by placing her arm over his shoulders to help her.

"Let's get out of here, Jack," Harry exclaimed.

Clarisse was in some pain as she clasped onto them while trying to maintain her flimsy footing.

This demon played with their minds in the most profound sense. At one point, you were led to believe Willow Court Asylum was a place of happy spirits filled with joy, song, and laughter of infants playing games all day. On the other hand, you were exposed to everything wrong with the asylum—the despair, pain, and agony of women crushed by the cruelty of the doctor entrusted with their care.

It was deliberately confusing and meant to create extremes in emotions to disorientate your mental state. And by homing into your inner fears, the demon figured it would be too much for the frail mind to handle. That was, who could withstand this level of torment?

In the past, mediums, squatters, and ghost tour participants had been sent screaming from Willow Court Asylum, vowing never to return. It was like opposite ends of the emotional spectrum, which could not be compartmentalized. Willow Court Asylum liked to pull you in different locations. That was how it dealt with anyone who meddled in its sinister past.

9 ROYAL DERWENT HOSPITAL

Clarisse lay in bed alone, pondering the previous day's event. It didn't surprise her that the infant spirits' innocence was a cover for their sinister ways. A deliberate act to lay marbles next to the entrance of the abortion room was a planned act. The dark spirits of Willow Court Asylum knew she was pregnant, and that made her a perfect target.

Harry tried to convince her not to participate in the paranormal investigation because of her pregnancy. He was happy to take on the assignment with Paranormal Jack Jr. and apply their technological smarts. He was keen to test the state-of-the-art tools and find evidence of the infant spirits. But Clarisse was stubborn and steadfastly refused, finding every angle to reassure him it was okay.

She lay in bed at Royal Derwent Hospital, a facility built

around the same time as Willow Court Asylum. It was an old hospital, refurbished over the years. It had an old-time charm and some character.

But Clarisse was not out of the woods. They were waiting for the obstetrician to arrive from Hobart to review her tests. They feared her unborn child may have been hurt as a trickle of blood was found on her sheets overnight. Never a good sign for an expecting mother. It also worried Harry to death. To think that her visit to Willow Court Asylum would put Clarisse and their child in harm's way played on his mind continuously.

She looked up instinctively to find an unexpected visitor waiting at the door—Father O'Connor. He was wearing black trousers and a standard black tab collar shirt. In his arms, he was holding a black cassock that would have kept him warm from the cold snap that had passed through the town.

"You've noticed they don't have a maternity ward in this hospital, my dear," he said in a gentle tone. He took a couple of steps into the room and pulled out the visitor's chair. "May I?" He raised his eyebrows.

His inviting demeanor made her feel comfortable.

"Oh yes, Father. They had to call the obstetrician from Hobart, about thirty miles away, and they said he would arrive later this afternoon. But it worries me having to wait so long."

Father O'Connor nodded and held his hands together. "The locals stopped coming to the maternity ward a long time ago; superstitious their child may be taken from them. Our history runs deep, you know. So they closed it to save money. It was a non-functioning maternity ward for years."

"So, I'm the first patient in a long time then?"

"Oh yes, pretty much. The Royal Derwent Hospital goes back a long time and was connected to Willow Court Asylum in the early days. Their histories have crossed paths many times." He took out his holy cross and laid it on his lap. "I came to say a prayer for you, to help you through this trauma, my dear." He looked at Clarisse with imposing eyes. "The marbles that caused you to fall down and hurt yourself was no accident, my dear."

"You mean it was deliberate?"

"It was a warning, Clarisse. I know evil can speak to you, that you hear the voices of the dead, see their spirits and, through a form of self-induced hypnotism, you can see the past."

Clarisse pondered Father O'Connor's comments. He was straight to the point and not mincing his words.

"Is there something about Willow Court Asylum you're

not telling us, Father? You've lived here all of your life, and we did capture you on camera before we arrived."

"So, it recorded my encounter?"

"Despite your attempts to confront the evil entity—and I don't think it was your first time—this demon is mighty powerful."

"You know it's a demon."

"I see evil, Father. Sometimes evil comes looking for me."

"Because you're a spirit hunter, and you're a threat to its existence."

Clarise shifted in bed to make herself comfortable then raised herself up the headboard. "So, what is it you want to confide in me, Father?"

He clasped his cross with both hands and mumbled to himself before placing his fingers across his lips. Sweat began to trickle down his face as his breathing became shallower and deeper.

"Well, tell me, Father. What is it? Am I in danger?"

"The demon wants your child, Clarisse. And next time, you won't be so lucky. The marbles on the floor and the voices of young infants playing in the hallway will be nothing compared to next time."

"Why does it want my child, Father?"

"Because that's what it does and has been doing for over

one hundred years. And make no mistake, you are a prize for the demon. To take the child of a formidable spirit hunter and hold you to ransom in the process ..." Father O'Connor stopped and took a deep breath. "Sorry, my dear, I don't mean to frighten you. It's a bad time to talk about these things. I apologize for hurting your feelings. I just wanted to check on you today and offer a prayer to you and the unborn child."

"It's okay, Father. Demons and I go back a long way. It's not the first time one's tried to cast doubt in my beliefs."

He smiled and sat back in his chair while making a big sigh. "Well, I'm glad we've had this conversation then, and an obstetrician will be coming to see you soon. Hobart is only thirty-five miles away. I'm sure you've just experienced a small knock, and that your baby is fine."

"But wait, Father," Clarisse said as she raised her hand to get his attention. "You haven't told me what's in the basement?"

"Maybe next time, my dear. I don't want to upset you in your condition."

"Can you stop trying to protect me all the time and tell me what's down there? Do you think I haven't seen evil before and stared it in the face? I know their ways—their trickery and lies, and how they set out to ruin lives and destroy families and communities. I've seen it all before and more often than you think."

Father Connor was about to leave the room when he stopped and turned toward her. "You really want to know?"

Clarisse nodded without saying a word.

He put his hands in his pockets and paced around the room, slowly thinking of the right words to describe the horrors in the basement. "When Willow Court Asylum opened in 1835 and became established in the colony, one of the first doctors to join the facility was a young, brash English doctor by the name of Marcus Pendergrass. Recently arrived from his mother country—Britain—he was just out of school and thought the new colony was the adventure he was looking for. In his early days at the mental asylum, he showed promise and smarts. He impressed his superiors with new techniques on managing patients for mental health issues."

"That may describe the design and the colors of Willow Court."

"Yes, my dear. Up until today, that facility was seen as ahead of its time in social engineering. You see, Dr. Pendergrass believed many patients could be rehabilitated back into the community and be less of a burden on the State. He introduced several new initiatives that proved to be successful. The lime-colored walls and the distinctive charm of the entrance to Willow Court that lead to separate private rooms and wonderful gardens were all his ideas."

"But something was not right?" Clarisse interjected impatiently.

"Hmm … There was another side to him, which took hold as he got older. And, by the time he was in his early forties, he started to become fascinated with complex procedures on childbirth. He believed he could find a way to save mother and child from certain death if they encountered complications." Father O'Connor paused for a moment to catch his breath. "His intentions were admirable at the time in cutting-edge obstetrics. But then he went mad and started experimenting on the patients from Ward C. Are you sure you want me to continue?"

Clarisse nodded. "Yes Father."

"Each time an experiment failed, he would become outraged, like a madman, and he would disappear into his experiment room. That's the basement at the entrance to Willow Court."

Clarisse took a deep breath and clutched her belly.

Father O'Connor felt tentative at first and held back until he built the courage to explain the remainder of the gruesome tale. "Many female patients died on the abortion table. Many fetuses were stillborn, and some may have survived had he been less careless and experimental."

"He knew his experiments could prove fatal to mother and child?"

"Clarisse, you're putting it mildly, my dear. He became a monster and a butcher of pregnant women. Some even went as far to say that ..."

"Say what, Father?"

"The devil had taken hold of Dr Pendergrass, that he sold his soul to evil so he could fulfill his experiments."

"He made a deal with the devil?"

"That's the folklore, but we will never know for sure."

"How do you know all this, Father?"

"Dr. Monserrat wrote a journal about his findings. They were kept secret for decades until, one day, they were released to the public."

"And the Catholic church was one of them?"

"Yes, the Catholic church sought the release of the diary. Remember, we have managed the beliefs and ensured God's will since the first convict arrivals at New Norfolk. Our church has been an integral part of New Norfolk for over a hundred and fifty years. We demanded a right to that report, and even though some government officials of the time tried to prevent us from getting a copy, we prevailed." Father O'Connor squinted. "Politics, you know. Sometimes you need to play bureaucrats at their own game ... as much as I dislike it."

Clarisse absorbed all the information then said, "I'm getting a feeling there's more to the story, Father."

"Yes, my dear, I know you can connect with the afterlife. The spirits come looking for you, and evil speaks to you. You're one of a kind. Many of the paranormal investigators who have tried and failed at Willow Court were glorified mediums. They thought they could get into what lurks in Willow Court, unravel the secret. Ha-ha ... And many left screaming. I've seen the devil that lurks in the corridors of that place on more than one occasion."

Clarisse tried to refocus Father O'Connor, as he was starting to become emotional. "So, you found something gruesome and horrific in Dr. Monserrat's report?"

Father O'Connor paused and took another deep breath while pacing around the room. "Yes, yes, I did. He reported that Dr. Jordan found a cluster of babies dead in the basement in 1878. Dr. Pendergrass had gone completely mad and had decided on a new experiment that required more than one newborn to complete the analysis."

"Oh my God ... That's horrible. I couldn't imagine such a thing."

"A cluster of babies found dead ... except one was found breathing and alive. Born in 1878. That child continued living in New Norfolk all their life until they passed away. Described as a recluse who didn't like to mingle too much, he would attend church every Sunday without fail at my parish and head into town for supplies. But, other than that, nobody was close enough to him—he had no friends."

"Did he have children? I'm assuming we're talking about generations that have grown up here?"

"He was married with one child. And yes, the family has lived in the area for generations. I suppose they have become part of the folklore, also."

"There's more to this story, isn't there?" Clarisse was poking Father O'Connor to tell more.

"Well, the folklore is he battled demons all his life. Not his own personal demons, as he was a rational man, but the one believed to possess Willow Court."

"He was a missionary carrying out God's work?"

"I've never thought of it that way, describing his purpose in life in that manner. But, I guess if you look deeply, perhaps that was his mission."

As Father O'Connor waved goodbye to Clarisse and was just about to leave, Harry and Paranormal Jack Jr. came rushing in. They were startled by Father O'Connor and unsure why he had come to visit Clarisse.

"Hello, Harry and Jack. I just came by to check on

Clarisse. It looks like she'll be okay."

Harry acknowledged him, not wanting to be rude. "Thanks for checking on Clarisse, Father. We had to organize an obstetrician from Hobart. He's on his way … should be here in an hour."

"Oh, that's great news!" Father O'Connor shook Harry's hand. "May the Lord bless you both."

Paranormal Jack Jr., who had a long connection with the Catholic church in Hartley, also thanked Father O'Connor for visiting Clarisse.

"Oh, Jack … I wanted to ask you something," Father O'Connor said in an impromptu manner.

"Sure Father, what is it?"

"Tell me, and be honest with me, on your first day at Willow Court, I heard you went to check out the basement."

"Yes Father, but it was locked. I couldn't get in."

"Hmm … But that's not what I mean. Did you feel or sense anything unusual?"

Paranormal Jack Jr. placed his hands in his pockets and looked down tentatively. His eyebrows moved up and down as he twitched his forehead. "I heard the voices of young children … playing and giggling. But that's not all."

"You sensed something that made you feel uneasy, didn't you?"

"Yes Father. It's hard to explain, but I felt a negative energy. It was like pain, anger, and sorrow, all packaged into one emotion. I don't know if that makes any sense."

"Oh, my son, I understand what you felt. There's misery in that room. A chamber of horrors, and that's why I lobbied to have it locked and closed to the public."

"It's practically fortified, and even the squatters couldn't break into it." Paranormal Jack Jr. nodded slightly. Then he shook Father O'Connor's hand and thanked him for passing by again.

He left the room while Harry, Clarisse, and Paranormal Jack Jr. all looked at each other.

"So, what was that about, Clarisse? Why was Father O'Connor here?"

Clarisse avoided the question altogether and glanced toward Harry with a provocative look. "Once I've been checked out from this hospital, Harry, I'm going back to Willow Court."

"Oh no, you're not, Clarisse. It's out of the question. Jack and I will complete the investigation. Remember, our brief is to find evidence of paranormal activity, not solve the curse of Willow Court."

Paranormal Jack Jr. butted into the conversation. "And this isn't Hartley, Clarisse; we're not here to exorcise whatever demon has occupied Willow Court and cleanse the spirits."

"Jack's right, you know. Tomorrow, we're meeting with Gary to give him an update, and I guess we need another evening at most to complete our work."

Clarisse screwed her lips up, and her cheeks tightened. She had an intense look on her face—scrunched forehead and clenched fists. "So, you want me to walk away after all that happened one hundred years ago? All those mothers who lost their child to a mad doctor? Just leave all that behind and walk out because you captured some sounds and pictures of paranormal activity?"

Harry and Paranormal Jack Jr. remained tight-lipped, knowing Clarisse was not happy, but neither did they want to make it a big deal.

"And Harry, have you told me everything you read in Dr. Monserrat's diary?"

"Well yeah, the most important parts, at least."

"You thought Dr. Monserrat was overemotional at the time … losing his marbles?"

"Well …"

"I thought so." Clarisse took a deep breath then exhaled in frustration. "That's what happens when a skeptic interprets paranormal events. You look at them in rational ways when it's anything but logical."

Harry didn't respond to Clarisse, wanting her to calm

down. He knew she could be tempestuous at times and of solid character.

Harry wanted to know if their baby was fine, that the fall hadn't caused any complications to Clarisse and their child. Chasing demons and exorcising evil had taken second place as to a soon-to-be father. He was looking at the world from a different perspective. Because, in the past, what Clarisse was suggesting was precisely how they approached the problem. They would have fought the demon in its own domain and worked out a way to exorcise the evil and save the community. She had put herself at risk on each occasion, whether at Hartley or Old Tailem Town. Even her first attempt at taking on an evil possession with the scarlet chair had caused her to be hospitalized. This time, the circumstances were different. She could not be the martyr to overcome the wickedness and immorality of the demon in the basement of Willow Court.

The next day, and before Harry picked up Clarisse from the Royal Derwent Hospital, he and Paranormal Jack Jr. went to Willow Court Asylum. They wanted to check the ghostbusting equipment and see what trails of energy had been left behind. They were particularly interested in the night vision equipment to see if they had captured paranormal activity. They were also conscious that Gary was meeting them straight afterward to see how things were progressing with the investigation. Like any mayor, he had heard about Clarisse's fall and wanted to make sure he followed through on his responsibilities to ensure their safety.

"The equipment's been moved." Paranormal Jack Jr. pointed to the night vision camera that had turned one-hundred-and-eighty degrees, now facing the wall. How long it had been that way was anyone's guess, and nothing could be recorded unless a ghost had appeared in front of the wall.

"The audio device is flashing red on the dial, which means it's still recording."

"So, where do we start, Harry?"

"Yeah, I'm more intrigued by the night vision camera. With any luck, we may have some images."

The night vision camera had a six-inch monitor fixed to the device for quick previewing. All Harry had to do was press the rewind button to the point where it had detected movement.

They both huddled around the camera as it stopped where it had captured the last movement—a timestamp.

"Looks like we got something, Jack."

"Yeah, I can't wait to see what's on it."

Harry pressed the play button as they eagerly awaited to

review the imagery.

In the background, children were playing. Two girls hand clapped and sang in rhyme.

> "*Lemonade, iced tea.*
> *Lemonade. (clap, clap, clap)*
> *Crunchy ice. (clap, clap, clap)*
> *Sip it once, (clap, clap, clap)*
> *Sip it twice. (clap, clap, clap)*
> *Turn around, (turn around)*
> *Touch the ground, (touch the floor)*
> *Kick your brother out of town! And stomp!"*

As soon as they finished that song, they played another handclap.

> "*Apple on a stick,*
> *Makes me sick,*
> *Makes my heartbeat two-forty-six,*
> *Not because you're dirty,*
> *Not because you're clean,*
> *Just because you kissed a boy behind the magazine,*
> *Girls, girls, wanna have some fun?*
> *Here comes Suzy with her hoop skirt on,*
> *She can wibble, she can wobble, she can do*

the splits,
But I betcha ten dollars, she can't do this.
Close your eyes and count to ten,
If you miss your start again,
1-2-3-4-5-6-7-8-9-10 ... "

While the girls played handclap, two boys engaged in a game of marbles as they flicked their aggies and allies out of a triangle by scoring points each time. They continued playing for another minute until they disappeared.

Harry and Paranormal Jack Jr. looked at each other in awe at the perplexing images of infant spirits having fun. But they also realized they had obtained evidence of the paranormal that was undeniable.

Then came the sound of child whispers. It was difficult to gauge if the whispers came from the camera as they appeared to fill the room. It sounded like a little girl whispering in your ear. But the sound was muffled, as though her lips were pressed against a microphone. The distortion of being so close created an echo effect that sounded like thunderous clouds.

This continued for around a minute until a child's image appeared, staring at the camera. Harry and Paranormal Jack Jr. were so startled that they took a step back to adjust their vision of the impulsive image.

She had shoulder-length, red curly hair, neatly parted down the middle. Her bright-blue pupils on a white background created a striking ice-cold sensation. She peered into the camera but didn't make any movement, though her eyelids flickered. It was a paradox of motionless and moving parts that made no sense.

Light reflected on one side of her face as it transitioned to dark, creating a vernacular of color and hue. Her eyes were surrounded by dark shadows, and her black lips accentuated the soft contours of her face. She was an attractive little girl, nevertheless.

It was followed by a creepy little girl talking directly at the camera while standing many feet away. It was the same little girl, although in full view this time. An orange hue surrounded her, as though a spotlight had been placed on the stage.

"I'm so scared; all I want to do is play with you.
Please come and play with me. I'm so lonely.
You're not afraid of the dark, are you?
Don't be afraid. Come with me.
I will show you how to play handclap and jumping rope.

And then I can show you how I play hide and seek.

Do you want to play hide and seek?

You hide, and I find you?

You're going to die in the basement.

Don't say I didn't warn you.

I know things about the basement that nobody knows.

Your Clarisse is going to die ...

I'm sorry. She is so beautiful and ready to have a child.

I'm alone and scared. I lost my mummy.

Can you help me find her, find her ...

Find her ... find her?"

Her final words echoed throughout the hallway and slowly phased out until it was quiet again. For a moment, there was nothing on view, but then came the ominous sound of a little boy calling for his mother.

It started off as a single tone then overlaid by the exact rendition over and over. It was spine-tingling as Paranormal Jack Jr. and Harry shook their shoulders and their stomachs churned. It was eerie and heartfelt, and it carried a sense of guilt. How could you not be affected? Harry couldn't help feeling a deep-seated desire to take the child in his arms and comfort him.

"Mummy ... Mummy ...
Mummy ... Mummy ...
Mummy ... Mummy ...
Where are you?"

Harry had seen enough of the infant spirits and their manifestations. He hastily turned off the camera, almost pushing the equipment onto the floor.

"What did the child say about Clarisse?" Paranormal Jack Jr. asked.

"You heard what the child said, Jack; do I need to repeat it?" Harry was short and uncomfortable.

"We have what we need. The paranormal evidence, I mean." Paranormal Jack Jr. tried to diffuse Harry's temperament. "But what about the audio recording? Shouldn't we listen to it?"

"Why would it be any different? Children playing games, singing songs, and trying to draw us into their world so that we can feel sorry for them. A front for the demon who uses them to confuse us. Playing with our inner emotions then taking advantage of our insecurity. Frighten us and cause accidents to remind us of its ability to hurt if we push too far. That's what demons do, right?"

"Clarisse told me you never believed in demons and, even up until now, you looked for rational solutions to the manifestations. Isn't that what the equipment is for? You're not just looking for evidence of a poltergeist, but you're hoping there's a logical explanation?" Paranormal Jack Jr. could read through Harry's motivations, and now it was time to confront him.

"Well Jack, I've changed. I never believed in poltergeists, ghosts, or demons. When I first met Clarisse, I thought it was a bit of fun, like the scarlet chair then meeting your dad. But things happened in Hartley that started to change my mind, and the same in Old Tailem Town. It wasn't a coincidence anymore, and I couldn't find logical explanations. I couldn't come to terms with the spirit world."

"And what about now and this inner conflict you have about whether spirits exist?"

Harry clasped his hands and looked down, almost embarrassed to admit he changed his point of view. "Jack, the reason why I agreed to this investigation ..."

"Yes, I know, mate. It's your final attempt to prove there are no spirits, and you invested heavily in the best equipment to do so. But what you forgot is that your equipment is only a tool, and whether you believe in spirits, ghosts, or demons comes down to your heart. You either feel them, see them for what they are, and accept they live in a parallel universe—it's that simple—or you don't."

Harry looked down and shrugged.

Paranormal Jack Jr. could sense he was feeling uncomfortable with the conversation.

"And that's the difference between you and Clarisse. She was born with those attributes. She never asked for them or wanted to be a spirit hunter. She never thought evil would speak to her and use her as a conduit. These are rare qualities that you're born with."

"And you, Jack? What about you? Are you like Clarisse, also?" Harry was defiant and testing.

"Huh, I wish I could be half as good as her. Yes, I have the same qualities, but Clarisse's perceptions are advanced and refined. For example, I can't self-meditate and see people's pasts like she does. And spirits don't necessarily speak to me with a sense of ease. I must work a lot harder at it. But, as for my dad, Paranormal Jack Sr. had those qualities, and he kept them to himself."

"Jack, your father was a good man, and I liked him a lot. And when he left this world, I was devastated. But I'm glad you're here. You're a good man."

Harry was taken emotionally by the voices of the infant spirits. They were deliberately angelic and designed to extract our inner emotions and pity for young children. It was because we were all children once.

The flood of memories came rolling in for Harry and

Paranormal Jack Jr.

A child without a mother, alone, and in the dark, is a compelling inner fear we all carry deep inside. We have all been lost once before, whether in a park or playground, and called out for Mummy, to find her suddenly reappear, making us feel safe again.

The infant spirits called out for their mummies every day, but they never turned up.

It was apparent the demon who controlled Willow Court Asylum and Ward C understood the power of human emotion. No matter who you were or how tough you thought you were, the gentle voice of children triggered an emotional reaction that was too much to bear for some people.

But there was also a greater sense of awareness because Harry was preparing for his first child with Clarisse. The thought that she could be in danger or harmed in any way made him want to pack up his equipment and leave. And if the issue was providing evidence for Gary, then their obligations had been met. They didn't need to stick around anymore. All he had to do was hand over the night vision and sound recordings to Gary, and they were done.

The problem was convincing Clarisse to leave. She was her own woman and didn't like being bossed around and told what to do. She was fiercely independent and had made that clear to him when they had first met. That was her character and what made her a formidable opponent to any evil that lurked in such places. And Harry was intelligent enough to know he could never change her. Neither did he want to. That was the side of her that he admired the most.

The conundrum was that evil spoke to Clarisse. Even if he left Willow Court Asylum for their next destination, evil could follow her. He had seen it at Old Tailem Town when Little Charlie's spirit followed them from Hartley, unbeknownst to them. He had latched on to Clarisse to seek a way out of the darkness and transition from the spirit world. It was a call for help, even though it was still playing out its sinister ways, living the life of a poltergeist.

As for now, Harry knew Clarisse was in danger if they continued with their investigation, and the voices had provided that warning. More so, the six month pregnancy could also be in trouble if the voices were to be taken seriously.

Was it scaremongering or a threat? What did the demon of Willow Court want with Clarisse's child? It was a perplexing question that made him feel uneasy.

10 THE EVIL SIGNATURE

Clarisse was happy she suffered no internal injuries from her fall, and her baby was fine. When the doctor had asked her about her incident, she told a white lie and felt guilty.

"I fell over during a paranormal tour of Willow Court," she had said.

The obstetrician, having grown up in the area, was well-versed in the superstitions and folklore of Willow Court Asylum. He commented that he wanted to complete the paranormal tour one day. However, his job kept him so busy that he couldn't ponder when he would be next available.

During the conversation, he explained to Clarisse the story of the cluster of babies that had died suspiciously in 1878. It seemed everyone who had grown up around New Norfolk was familiar with the story. He also said he couldn't understand why local women didn't want to deliver their babies in this hospital.

"It has all the facilities for women to be cared for during delivery. It's on par with the hospital in Hobart, and it would save me having to travel here for emergencies," he said.

Nevertheless, he left Clarisse with his details should her condition change or she needed to discuss anything over the phone.

As she lay in bed, a feeling of relief took over her. She was finally clear of any medical condition affecting her baby or herself. It had been a close call, and she was lucky. The obstetrician had told her that she was fortunate to have fallen on her back, which cushioned the fall from the baby and thereby sustaining no injuries.

As she reached for a glass of water on her side table, she saw an ominous shadow from the corner of her eyes but couldn't make it out. Clarisse shook her head and blinked excessively to make sure she wasn't seeing things. Then the realization came flooding in that she knew this ghastly image well.

"So, we meet again, my dear." He dipped his hat and crossed his legs while seated in the visitor's chair.

"It can't be you. I thought you were …"

"Say it. That I was condemned to the depths of hell?" It

was the demon from Hartley, speaking its usual cockney accent.

"Yes, that's right. From the depths of hell."

"Well, demons don't die; we just move on to another place. But I was lucky my demon master had a soft spot for me and accepted my plan for Willow Court."

Clarisse was curious but remained calm without being overawed by its presence. "You knew about Willow Court back in Hartley?"

"Oh yes, my dear. I sort of stumbled upon it, to be exact. And I've got to hand it to you … what a formidable opponent you turned out to be. I watched you at Old Tailem and how Little Charlie followed you there. He liked you, and even though he couldn't express it, he wanted you to free him from his cursory existence."

"So, why do you follow me, demon? Why not someone else?"

"Hmm … Do I need to explain it? Because you're unique and represent a challenge. Not many mortals can do what you do. You can speak to evil, and the afterlife can speak to you. You were able to enter a self-hypnotic state and tap into a spirit's past. You can feel the energy fields and vibrations of spirits around you from afar. Do you want me to go on?"

Clarisse adjusted her posture and looked steadfastly at

the demon. "And I know you well enough to know that you're a charmer and a conversationalist, but that doesn't explain why you're here."

The demon pulled out a pipe and lit it, ensuring he inhaled the first puffs to get the fire burning the apple-scented tobacco. "Willow Court Asylum was empty with a bunch of infant spirits wandering around endlessly for generations. The last demon was cast to hell, as his masters became sick of his incompetence—the afterlife repeating itself day after day with the same routine … It was getting boring. It was like a video being played repeatedly with the same start and end."

"So, you saw an opportunity?"

"Oh yes. I took the young ones under my wing and showed them the ropes. Did you like the marbles and the jumping rope routine?"

When Clarisse didn't answer, he continued, "A mother struck a deal with the last demon to be together with her son in the afterlife. She was supposed to follow her side of the bargain and look after the other children."

"Like a nanny?" Clarisse interrupted.

"Yeah, something like that. But in a way, that cluster of children are only there because of a crazed doctor who decided to turn Willow Court Asylum into a big experiment." The demon paused and took a puff of his pipe then exhaled. Although there was no visible smoke, the apple fragrance filled the room. "You have discovered his name was Dr. Pendergrass, a leading obstetrician but also a psychotic man. In fact, whoever was put in charge of the asylum had totally misread him. He is the one who should have been committed."

"It still doesn't explain why you're here, demon."

"Yes, let's get back and focus on your original question. I do have a habit of wandering off in all directions. My demon master says I talk too much and give information away too easily. It lets my guard down. But I only do that with you, my dear, and nobody else."

The demon stood up from his chair while holding onto a cane. "You know I see the future, although I can't alter it. I can see events playing out in advance, but that doesn't mean they end up that way. Demons only get a general sense of direction where things may lead to."

"So, you know half the future, then?

"Hmm … That's a good way of putting it, my dear. And, as for *your* future, I'm afraid the obstetrician who examined you is an old, drunken fool. Oh yes, he forgot to tell you the part where he spends more time on the grog these days. It means he's not as sharp as he used to be and misses things."

"What are you suggesting, demon?" Clarisse's throat

dried up and became sticky as she swallowed, and her stomach curled from the tension.

"In less than seven days, the true nature of your fall will start to affect you. Your obstetrician didn't review the scans properly because he was tired and in a rush to get back to Hobart for the horse race. Oh yes, I forgot to mention he's a gambler, too."

Clarisse started to tense up and gripped her hands while curling her feet.

"By the time they detect the internal bleeding in your womb, it will be too late, and your child will succumb to your wounds."

Clarisse gulped because she knew how this demon operated. In Hartley, it had accurately predicted the death of several people, including Paranormal Jack Sr.

"But I can save you and the baby. You know I have the power. If you agree …"

"Another one of your blackmail attempts, demon?" Clarisse was short and straight to the point.

The demon smirked as he flippantly raised both hands. "Yes, I will let your child live, and then his soul becomes mine. He will join the infant spirits as the new kid on the block. They won't mind a new friend. In fact, some of them are starting to call you mummy already."

"They want me to be their mother?"

"Well, the current one Abbey, is useless and only cares for her own son. So, I suppose there's an opening for you, if you wish. Then you can be together for eternity."

Clarisse remained silent. It was too much information too soon for her.

The demon blew out his pipe, placed it in his pocket, buttoned up his patterned nineteenth-century coat, and tipped his hat toward Clarisse. "No need to make a decision now, my dear. Your time will come, and you'll come calling for me, begging me to save your baby at all costs. G'day, my dear. Oh, and don't think about calling that drunken fool who calls himself a doctor to check on your internal bleeding. He won't find it."

The demon left the room, leaving Clarisse unsure of what to do next. She had been discharged from the hospital, and Harry and Paranormal Jack Jr. were on their way to pick her up. They had a meeting scheduled with Gary at the council chambers to provide an update and show the evidence captured from the night vision and the audio recording devices. Harry was also bringing the spirit box to provide extra confirmation of paranormal activity. It was a mountain of proof, and hopefully, their mission was accomplished—having met the paranormal investigation obligations.

At the council chambers' office, they were greeted by

the charismatic Gary Charlton. He offered them tea, coffee, and locally made biscuits from the bakery around the corner. He was in a jovial mood, keen to learn about their findings.

"So, how did it all go?" Gary asked with a big smile. "Except for your fall, Clarisse, I suspect everything went according to plan. How are you feeling, anyway?"

Clarisse shuffled in her seat to get comfortable and took hold of her cup of tea. "I've been cleared by the obstetrician from Hobart. He said I was lucky I fell on my back and not on my belly." She sipped her tea then sighed. "I guess it was my instinct to fall that way—a mother's intuition, I suppose."

"Oh, that drunken fool from Hobart," he whispered to himself. Although Gary was pleased Clarisse was not seriously hurt, and her child was clear of any complications, he wanted to get into the evidence.

"So, what do you have for me? Tell me about your experience at Willow Court."

Paranormal Jack Jr. plugged the night vision camera into the monitor so that they could all get a good look.

"We found evidence of paranormal activity, and it wasn't like anything we've seen before," Harry said.

"It's a playground of infant spirits; about four of them from seven years of age to around twelve. They have a minder, and we believe her name is Abbey."

"Hmm … That's a good start, and it may explain some of the sightings by people over the years, particularly when the paranormal tours were in full swing—the sounds of children playing in the Ward C and the ominous figure of a shadowy woman."

Harry nodded and continued with his explanation. "The old abortion room in particular, is laced with evil, and we felt the presence of dark spirits."

"Horrible things happened in that room," Paranormal Jack Jr. interrupted.

Clarisse was becoming fidgety and impatient. Not to mention, she could see through Gary's façade. "And of course, there's Dr. Monserrat's diary, which I believe you are fully conversed in and didn't share with us."

"I'm not sure what you're alluding to, Clarisse." Gary's mood changed instantly while being pressed.

"Well, why don't you tell him, Harry?"

Harry sighed as he reached for his computer bag, retrieving a lengthy document of at least a hundred pages of Dr. Monserrat's notes. Then he slammed it onto the table. "Clarisse is referring to this document. Oh, and by the way, it's well-known to Father O'Connor, too, and I suspect many other locals who have grown up in this town."

Gary didn't overreact, even though he was being challenged. He took a hold of his cup of coffee and held it in the palm of his hands while he looked across the room, avoiding eye contact with everyone. "Okay, yes, I do know about Dr. Monserrat's diary. It's a public document for those who can manage to locate it. There are many locals, including Father O'Connor, who have read every page of that document more than once."

"So, why didn't you provide us a copy for prereading or research before our investigation?" Clarisse pressed.

"It was a council decision when I sought approval for the investigation." Gary placed his coffee on the table then leaned forward on his desk. "There are councilors who have deep roots in this town that go back for over a hundred years. In fact, one of them can trace their ancestry to a mental health patient who resided at Willow Court." Gary reclined in his seat and folded his arms over his chest. "We were not trying to be sneaky; you know."

"At around 1878, a cluster of babies were found dead, and one survived. Whether he was meant to live or not, we're unsure. Abbey made a deal with the devil so that her child would live through childbirth and keep her baby until a certain age. It was ten years, I believe, before the devil took his soul. The child and mother were going to die during a high-risk operation performed by Dr. Monserrat, who claimed it was a miracle." Harry stared into Gary's eyes while lifting the document. Then he slapped it on the table, too. "It's all in here Gary, for everyone to read."

Harry then pressed play on the video recording, and Father O'Connor appeared on the screen. It was the scene where he had visited Ward C and had a confrontation with the demon.

"You can see clearly from this recording that Father O'Connor has confronted something evil." Harry looked directly at Gary with a forceful stare. "I don't think he was at Willow Court just for fun. He went there to confront whatever evil lurks there."

Gary watched on as Father O'Connor's confrontation with evil played out in front of him, caught by surprise that they had managed to find this evidence.

"So, what are you not telling us?" Clarisse asked. "There's more, isn't there?"

Everyone in the room turned to Gary, focused on his response.

He took his time and remained calm as he thought about his reaction.

"Okay, let's hold off on the video recordings for a moment and let me explain something very personal to me." Gary took a deep breath then swallowed. "The baby you refer to as the only survivor of a cluster of babies found dead was my great-grandfather. I'm a descendent of that tragic event. And yes, his mother was a mental patient of Willow Court Asylum.

"That also means I'm a direct descendant of the mental patient who apparently was diagnosed with a severe bipolar condition. And you know what? Today, she could have been treated with medicine and other therapies and lived a normal life rather than having been locked up in the private ward."

"I understand it wasn't easy for you to share that with us, Gary," Clarisse said in a peaceful tone. In Gary's eyes, she could see it was a touchy subject. It was kept in the family and on a need-to-know basis, like most locals who had a connection to Willow Court Asylum.

Although they were satisfied with his explanation, Gary continued to provide more.

"My father, who was born in 1942, God bless his soul, was a paranormal investigator like all of you. As a child, I heard my parents discussing his forays into Willow Court Asylum. Sometimes, he would stay overnight and come back mentally exhausted. He would keep to himself for days until he was able to recoup."

"Did he ever tell you why he was spending so much time at Willow Court?" Clarisse asked.

"Despite many attempts to get information from him

about his experiences at Willow Court, he would immediately shut down and not say a word. It was like a taboo subject, and we never spoke about it." Gary took a sip of his coffee then sat back in his seat. "Just before his passing, he told me everything one night while I was at his bedside. It was just my father and me as he held my hand and described the attempted exorcism in the basement at Willow Court. A couple of days later, after he passed away, I found a journal between a stack of books on his bookshelf." Gary's eyes were watery as he took a tissue and wiped his face.

"Have you read his journal?" Harry asked.

"My father was not an educated man, so his notes are hard to decipher; more a series of words and short sentences that don't really make sense. But before he passed away, he spent a lot of time at the church and got to know Father O'Connor very well. I guess they talked a lot about his experiences at Willow Court. He never set foot there again after the attempted exorcism and wanted nothing more to do with that place. But, by that time, he had already been affected."

"So, they attempted to exorcise the evil at Willow Court?" Clarisse asked, trying to get him to tell more.

"Yes, they did."

"There must be something in his diary that stood out,

that one thing that may bring us closer to the possession of Willow Court," Harry said.

Gary was not forthcoming as he played with his pen, flicking it continuously. In his own mind, he thought he might have said too much about his family secrets.

"We would like to know, Gary. Any clues or information will help us complete our project," Clarisse told him.

"Oh, but you have already provided me the evidence I asked for. That's all council needs for now. Your work is done if the evidence stacks up."

"Yes, but we can't just leave it like this. We need your help to—"

"Help to do what? Exorcise the poltergeists that have occupied that place for over a hundred years? Do you think you'll be the first ones to have tried?" It was a slip of the tongue by Gary.

Everyone was silent as they waited for Gary to regain his composure and share the rest of his story. Paranormal Jack Jr. shook his legs underneath the table while Harry sat back in the chair with his legs crossed. Clarisse took another sip of her tea while holding the warm cup in her palms. It was not the first time they'd had to contend with a local who was reluctant to share valuable information.

"What about the exorcism, Gary? How did your father

explain their attempt to cleanse the place?"

Gary placed his hands over his face and rubbed his eyes. "Do you really want to know what happened in that basement with my dad and Father O'Connor? Oh, and I'm not surprised the old man hasn't told you anything. Father O'Connor is very tight-lipped about anything to do with Willow Court. He's the one who argued incessantly to stop the paranormal investigation at a public hearing with the council."

"Yes, why don't you share the story with us," Harry said as Clarisse and Paranormal Jack Jr. nodded in support.

Gary placed his hand on his chin and sighed reluctantly. Then he took a deep breath and sat back in his chair as he commenced the recounting of his father's exorcism with a flashback of events.

11 WHAT EVIL LURKS BENEATH

The Exorcism 1982

Lindsay Charlton was no stranger to Willow Court, as he shared a bloodline going back to 1878 when his grandfather had faced evil as a baby. The only survivor of a cluster of children who had died under a savage tirade of Dr. Pendergrass and his convoluted experiments from hell. But, why had his grandfather survived while the other babies had confronted death? It was a question that plagued the family line for over a century. They felt dogged by the mystery and the unknown circle of guilt because his grandfather had been the only one to have survived without a plausible explanation.

Lindsay was a religious man and a staunch Catholic who spent weekends helping Father O'Connor with mass and other events on the religious calendar. He was the only man

Lindsay confided in about his terrible nightmares that seemed to be getting worse each year. He would wake up in the middle of the night with the faces of dead fetuses in his dreams. It was enough to drive any man crazy. He would be dripping in sweat with the sheets removed from his bed. That was until Lindsay had had enough and wanted to know why his family had been cursed. He decided to take matters into his own hands. So, with the help of Father O'Connor, they decided to tackle the evil head-on at Willow Court Asylum, where it had all started in 1878.

They knew from mediums who had visited Willow Court Asylum that it was seeded in the basement. This was the location where Lindsay's grandfather had been found alive by Dr. Jordan, in a pool of blood and slime that had dripped off the operating table and onto the floor, like a leaking tap. Discarded and thought dead by the mad doctor until he had been found barely alive, clinging to life with the slimmest of margins.

Dr. Monserrat had openly stated in his diary that it was a miracle Lindsay had survived and only a stroke of fortune had kept him alive. Had the excellent Dr. Jordan arrived an hour later, he wouldn't have lived.

Had it been divine intervention that had saved his grandfather from the deadly hands of Dr. Pendergrass and his evil experiments?

Lindsay looked on as Father O'Connor tried desperately to control his emotions. He thrust the old skeleton key into the mortice lock of the basement door, fixated on one thing only—to confront his deepest fears that lived in that room. Just being in Ward C of Willow Court Asylum was enough to set off an emotional reaction—to get even with the devil in there.

"The demon knows we're here," Father O'Connor said. He was holding his cross in one hand and a small bottle of holy water in the other. Although he was composed, the sacred water rattled in his hand.

Lindsay looked back at him as his eyes filled with sadness for all the victims who had lost their lives to the wicked Dr. Pendergrass. "The demon mustn't sense any fear, or it will take advantage. We come armed with God's word, filled with the Holy Spirit. We're strong, Father. Don't fear the evil that has tormented us for over a century."

Father O'Connor didn't respond. He knew Lindsay was right, because the only way to defeat a demon was not to expose your worst fears. Demons had an uncanny way of measuring your apprehension and using it to their advantage.

Lindsay turned the key quickly until he heard the click

of the mortice lock disengaging. Then he raised his foot and kicked the door open as he shoned his lantern into the room.

He placed his hands over his mouth. The room smelled like it had been untouched for a hundred years; a putrid stench that was not from this time and had carried over from generations.

"Is this what spirits smell like?" Father O'Connor asked.

"It's the signature of evil you are smelling, Father. They all have a different odor. It's how we identify them."

Father O'Connor sensed the evil in the air—the rotting moisture of death and the blood curdling screams of babies and their mothers who had died in this den of horrors.

"So, now you hide from us, demon? Behind the pitch-black curtains of your own hell!" Lindsay called out. "Show yourself, you scum of the Earth and murderer of mothers and children!"

Father O'Connor lifted his cross into the air and splashed the room with holy water that landed on the blood-speckled floor. The sprinkles hit the floor, evaporating instantly and steaming into the air. It was a clear sign of an evil presence in the room.

Lindsay couldn't help looking at the floor next to the operating table where the original droplets of bloodstains had soaked into the timber floor like a sponge, over the years, creating a tapestry of pain.

"How many innocent mothers and babies did you take to their deaths in this room, you cursed monster?" Lindsay called out as he scoured the room with his lantern, waiting for the face of evil to show itself.

The door behind them slammed shut, causing Father O'Connor to drop his cross. It had been a loud thump that prompted the room to vibrate then rattle.

"It's the devil in the room," Father O'Connor said.

Without them realizing it, the demon had been standing behind the door the whole time, watching their every move. Rising seven feet tall, on hooves, half-animal and half-man, with bat-like wings spread to accentuate its size, it growled so loudly, like a rumble, they had to place their hands over their ears. The demon's tongue flickered like a snake. Its long, elongated hands and three-inch, sharp nails fiddled like a magician introducing its next trick. Its eyes fused in red fire represented the only color of this black monster from hell.

In a coarse, baritone voice, the demon raised its hand and said, "It was easy to get Dr. Pendergrass to perform those acts for my own pleasure. After a while, he liked watching babies and mothers die in this room. And all in the name of science. Nothing like a madman running an asylum, don't you think?"

Father O'Connor scrambled to pick up his cross then raised it toward the demon and started to pray to exorcise the devil.

"Oh, that's futile, man of God!"

The cross suddenly caught fire, burning his hand before dropping to the floor. Father O'Connor screeched from the pain and clasped his burnt hand.

"Those symbols don't work in here. This is my world. I control what goes in this basement."

Father O'Connor looked to Lindsay in despair, knowing that reciting the prayer of exorcism was futile. The demon was too powerful, and they had come under attack unless they had another way of fighting the devil.

"Oh, and don't think Dr. Pendergrass acted alone. He had helpers. Delaney, the head nurse, organized the babies from the maternity ward. The sex-deprived Irish maintenance man, who couldn't fix anything if his life depended on it, raped the women. A triage of evil doing all my work to please me. How's that for power and control?"

The demon clapped its hand, and a burst of energy, in the form of a vibration, lifted Lindsay and Father O'Connor off the ground. They levitated for thirty seconds before being hurled to the floor. Father O'Connor landed on his back with a *thump*, feeling the pain resonate all the way to his shoulders.

"I was running the asylum, not the doctors!" the demon exclaimed in a burst of anger.

Lindsay did not fear the presence of the demon. He looked directly into its fiery eyes, standing firm, with his arms by his sides and clasping his hands into fists. "We didn't come here to negotiate with you, demon. You haven't had a kill in over a century, and that must make your blood-thirsty tongue shrivel in pain. No babies, no curdling blood and shrieks of pain to satisfy your hunger. You live a lonely, cursed existence in your own self-executed capture in chains, right here in this image of hell you've created for yourself.

"I don't need to do anything but walk away, shut the door, and let you rot for another century. Make your empty stomach churn, and your head spin from your inability to kill again." Lindsay had learned the devil had no influence, no helpers, and no madmen to guide through and execute the terror it needed to sustain itself. In a way, it had created its own dungeon within the four walls of the basement where it lay bound and captured by its own creation.

The demon laughed as it tried to hide its weakness. "But I will reward you handsomely if you become my aide. Bring me another mother and her unborn child. You'll have all the riches you could imagine. Anything you want!" The demon had shriveled into the corner of the room and had become a shadow of itself. "Well, what do you say? Join me … forget your God. What do you want? Women, money, power, to live like a king? That's easy for me. Just say the word."

Father O'Connor tugged on Lindsay's arm. "We need to leave this room now. There's nothing we can do here." He sensed the danger of a demon that was used to getting its way.

Lindsay nodded, having realized the demon could not be defeated in its own den. Still, it could be imprisoned in the basement of horrors without go-betweens. So, the best strategy was to leave it dormant in the basement, devoid of external influence. At this point, the best the demon could do outside the confines of the basement was only to scare people.

Father O'Connor lifted his lantern and was captured by the low pitch sounds of church bells. It was uncanny to hear the announcement of the call to prayer in the devil's den. It was the standard quarter-hour bell sequence for most Christian churches, not just Catholic. Described as the Westminster Chimes, it was immediately recognizable.

He looked toward Lindsay, hoping he could explain the bells, but he just shrugged—it didn't make sense to him, either. Then, as they looked around to see where the church bells came from, four children of different ages appeared. The youngest must have been six years old and the oldest, a girl of at least twelve years. The children circled them and skipped in a counterclockwise manner. They were emotionless and didn't show their faces as they looked directly ahead. Around and around they danced until the chants of children singing filled the room with a nursery rhyme.

> *"Ring around the rosie.*
> *A pocketful of posies.*
> *A-tishoo, a-tishoo.*
> *We all fall down.*
> *The king has sent his daughter,*
> *To fetch a pail of water.*
> *A-tishoo, a-tishoo.*
> *We all fall down."*

Lindsay was caught in an emotional bent. Perhaps this was what the demon wanted to press upon him. To remind him that the four children were the cluster of babies who had died when his grandfather had survived. And he owed his life to him as the descendant of the only child to have survived the horrors in this room.

Had Dr. Pendergrass been aware that one child had

survived and prevented the curse from realizing its wrath? The descendant of the fifth child, required to complete the malediction, was now standing in the devil's den as the children danced around him, scoffing and tormenting his mind.

He placed his hands over his ears as the gregarious sounds of the infants repeated, faster and faster, louder each time. A cacophony of children's voices mixed into one distinctive speech.

Confused by it all, the children began walking around the room quicker, like a spinning wheel, as Lindsay became disoriented. The distorted images of the children became imprinted into his mind as he desperately tried to shake away the blurring, ghastly images. But they continued circling him like a merry-go-round until their images became distorted.

Father O'Connor had to act quickly as the spell took hold of Lindsay, taking over his senses. He grabbed Lindsay by the shoulder then pulled him toward the door, bracing him tightly while he used his other hand to turn the doorknob.

The demon, angered by their retreat and reluctance to join his pack of cursed evil incarnations, growled as it raced across the room in the form of a dark shadow. Objects started flying in their direction, and anything that was not fixed to something pelted them.

Father O'Connor raised his hand to protect his face as an object struck the wall next to them. Books, a chair, operating utensils, empty glass bottles, and boxes filled with leftover clothing smashed against the wall, and sharp operating tools pierced the door next to them, narrowly missing their heads.

The demon growled once more with a baritone hiss as the room shook with an intense vibration.

Lindsay clung onto Father O'Connor, unaware of what was happening. He was delirious and delusional as he mumbled with his eyes drooping and barely managing to keep his head upright.

Father O'Connor then opened the door, allowing enough of a gap to get out of the devil's den. And, as he closed the door behind them, a piercing instrument, once used by Dr. Pendergrass for his gruesome procedures, penetrated the six-inch thick wooden door. It was meant to display the demon's anger toward them. A close call for both, considering that instrument had been meant for them from a monster with no scruples, used to getting its way, and it had nearly succeeded.

Father O'Connor locked the door by fidgeting the key into the mortice lock and turned it shut … *click, click*. He pledged never to return and never to let anyone step foot in the basement again. He needed to convince the town locals that keeping the demon locked inside the basement, without the ability to coax, was the key to keeping it at bay.

Father O'Connor and Lindsay had at least confirmed the devil's curse, and it was incomplete. It needed five unborn children to possess the town and unleash its powers. Any other soul taken by the demon, who was not a newborn, whether an older child, a mother, or a man, could not complete the curse.

Through the scriptures in the Bible, Father O'Connor studied the *Five Points of Calvinism*—the number five representing death. That was the purpose of the curse—to regain the Five Points of Calvinism and the symbol of death so it could reign untouched and beyond reproach, tormenting and destroying lives throughout the town and beyond. The inception of evil that had limitless power and no boundaries.

But, when Lindsay's grandfather had been found alive and barely breathing, those plans had been thrown into disarray, and the devil's curse had not been complete. Now it roamed the asylum, waiting for the right child candidate.

It couldn't be just any child either, making its task harder. It had to be one worth taking and considered a prize. The child had to come from a mother who had spiritual prowess and strong faith in God.

It wasn't a case of just turning up at the maternity ward and negotiating with a mother on the impending death of a child. The survival rates of mothers with birth complications had changed. Under challenging circumstances, there were cesareans, as high forceps deliveries were a thing of the past. In a way, the technology and techniques used today had rendered evil less opportunity.

12 THE FIVE POINTS

Present Day

There was a hurried knock at the main entrance of the presbytery of Saint Peter's church. As Father O'Connor looked on from the hallway, he could see the subtle outlines of three people through the ornate, stained-glass window.

"Who is it?" he called out. There were no church events planned, and he was done for the day. Unsure why anyone would be visiting so late in the afternoon, he waited for an answer before he attended to the door.

"It's me, Clarisse, and I'm with Paranormal Jack Jr. and Harry. Can we talk to you, Father?" He was a frail, old man, and so it took him a while to reach the main entrance as he shuffled along the hallway in his slippers.

"How can I help you?" he called out, not wanting to be bothered at this time of day and feeling annoyed.

"We had a chat with Gary about Willow Court, and we thought you could help with some information," Clarisse responded.

He unfastened the latch and bolt before slowly opening the door. The door was so fortified with security locks that one would think he was expecting a break-in.

As he opened the door to full view, he noticed the glowing white teeth of Clarisse. She peered into his eyes, projecting a look of innocence.

"Sorry to bother you at this time of day Father, but we need to ask you some questions about the basement at Willow Court. We're trying to conclude our investigation, but there are some gaps we need to close off. Gary thought you could help us fill in the missing pieces?"

"Hmm …" Father O'Connor grunted while clearing his throat. He knew why they had turned up and wasn't too keen on sharing the secrets of Willow Court. However, he was a realist and had understood when Gary called for the paranormal investigation that it would lead to him at some point. Therefore, their appearance was not a surprise.

"Why don't you take a seat over there in the study, and I'll be right with you? I've something of interest that may help with our conversation."

He returned with a document bound in old, cream-colored paper with a red ribbon tied around it.

Clarisse was curious and wondered why the document was of such value to him and how he had managed to get hold of it.

They all sat in the comfortable, antique chesterfield chairs; relics of when the church had first been built but still in surprisingly good condition.

"What's that document?" Paranormal Jack Jr. asked, wanting to get straight to the point.

"Well these, my dear children, are known as the Five Points of Calvinism. These doctrines are named for the theological stances taken by the reformer, John Calvin."

They all look confused.

Clarisse frowned and squinted her eyes. Harry was listening but was uncertain what to make of it.

"It looks ancient. I'm assuming it's been with the church for some time?" Harry asked.

"Huh, this document has a long history." Father O'Connor was poised while he laid the document on the side table in front of them. "It was found by Dr. Monserrat around 1880, in a metallic box to have been specifically made for it. It belonged to one of his patients in Ward C. It was rumored to have arrived with the first batch of convict settlers in New Norfolk from Mother England.

They were a superstitious lot back then."

"How did it get into the church's hands?" Paranormal Jack Jr. asked.

"That I'm not too sure about. But it was already here before I arrived and apparently before my predecessor." Father O'Connor rubbed his eyes and yawned. "Excuse me. It's been a long day."

"Well, what a surprise to find a document like that with so much history." Clarisse appreciated the value of such documents from her previous experiences in other Australian ghost towns.

"Hmm … I knew you would like it. Let me explain to you in layman's terms what messages it entails so we can all understand it.

"The Five Points of Calvinism are commonly known by theologians, and those who follow the scripture, as TULIP.

"I'm assuming TULIP stands for something, Father?" Clarisse asked.

"Oh yes, these are the five points:

"Total Depravity (we're so messed up by sin we need Gods help),

Unconditional Election (God chose Christians to be his people),

Limited Atonement (Jesus died on the cross for Christians only),

Irresistible Grace (what happens during salvation when you're summoned to be a Christian and made anew), and

Perseverance of the Saints (you'll grow with Jesus until the end of your lives)."

They all looked at each other, confused and not sure what to say. Harry shrugged, looking bewildered.

"Let me explain further," Father O'Connor said. "In dealing with the Five Points of Calvinism, it's fitting that five is the number of death. Just as it takes no keen intellect to see that five is the Biblical number of deaths, so no insight is necessary, other than an ability to read the Bible."

"So, the number five is an important number?" Clarisse asked as she shuffled in her chair and leaned forward. She was trying to keep things simple for Harry. "There were four babies in the cluster that were meant to die at Willow Court at the hands of the insane Dr. Pendergrass, with Abbey's baby being a fifth."

"And one survived," Father O'Connor said. "So, the devil's work was incomplete. And ever since, it's been looking for a fifth child to complete the curse." Father O'Connor rested back in his chair and nodded.

"What about your exorcism with Lindsay?" Clarisse pressed, knowing Father O'Connor would find her question uncomfortable.

"I know Gary has told you the story of Lindsay and me. It was bound to come out during the investigation. He did warn me."

Clarisse nodded and smiled. "I would like to know more about the number five and why it's the number of evil."

"You are a curious one." Father O'Connor gazed at him. "Gary warned me you would be inquisitive, too."

He sighed. "Let me explain the best way I can. The number five is referenced in the Bible many times. Satan, the angel of death, is the fifth cherub, and the first man dies in Genesis 5:5. In Acts 5:5, Ananias dies after being asked five questions about his sin. Paul was whipped five times, and Jesus Christ had five wounds." Father O'Connor took a deep breath then continued. "In Revelation, Chapter Five, we see the lamb that was slain. During the Tribulation, locusts will torment men for five months until they seek death. When the fifth seal is opened, John saw the souls of their slain. There were five men stoned in the Bible who died."

Father O'Connor took another deep breath and clasped his hands. "The greatest chapter in the Bible on death, describing two men whose deaths affected all humanity, is Romans Chapter Five. Even the word 'death' contains five letters. When David went forth to kill the giant Goliath, he carried with him five smooth stones—"

"I think I understand, Father. The demon is trying to unlock the power of the five points so it can grow in strength."

"Yes, but there are rules with the five points."

"Can you clarify, Father?" Clarisse asked.

"It must be five newborn children at the time of confinement. If the demon takes your soul later in life, it does not count."

"That may explain why the demon refused Dr. Monserrat's offer to take his soul in exchange for Abbey's child?" Harry was referring to the notes that he had read.

Father O'Connor nodded and tilted his head to the side. "Yes, his soul held no value to the demon. And to make matters more complicated, the fifth child must be a chosen infant, not just any child.

"How will it know?" Clarisse was digging deeper.

"When the fifth infant has arrived, it will know." Father O'Connor yawned again.

"And unleash a curse on New Norfolk and its people. That will lead to eternal misery. And who knows where the boundaries are and whether we can stop it? After New

Norfolk, it can extend its power beyond and free itself from the basement."

"How do we defeat the evil?" Paranormal Jack Jr. asked.

"Oh, you don't need to worry about that. Your job was to find evidence of paranormal activity, not to find information on the infant spirits, how many, their ages, and the limits to their power." Father O'Connor replied, fidgeting with his cross.

"But I learned something, Father, that you may not be aware of," Clarisse interrupted.

Father O'Connor waited patiently for an explanation with clasped hands while he shifted his position in the chair.

"The abortion chair has powers. I can tap into it and learn more about the devil's curse, its powers, and find out why the five points are the center of its plan."

"This isn't the scarlet chair, Clarisse," Harry interjected immediately, "where you defeated the demonic curse that plagued your family for hundreds of years. We're dealing with evil on a different level. This demon is ten times more powerful." He paused for a moment and took a deep breath as his face turned red and his cheeks tensed up from the thought. "Have you forgotten you're six months pregnant?"

"He's right you know, my dear. You put yourself and

your child at risk by reading the thoughts of the demon. I know evil speaks to you Clarisse, and you connect with the afterlife. That's why we brought you here—so we could get the evidence we needed … but not to put yourself in danger like that."

They all looked at each other, waiting for someone to make the first comment. There was dead silence in the room.

Harry looked down to the floor and placed his hands over his eyes. Paranormal Jack Jr. sat back with his arms crossed. And Father O'Connor kept on looking toward Clarisse with a solemn expression.

"I've been working on something that may help us resolve this problem." Harry's words broke the silence as everyone looked toward him. "I've been developing a new tool. It's in a beta stage but ready to go."

"Well, out with it, Harry," Paranormal Jack Jr. called out like an excited schoolboy. "What is this new toy of yours?"

"We don't need to tap into the energy of the abortion chair—that's too risky. And I think the devil's smart enough to point us in that direction."

"Because it knows it will have the upper hand?" Clarisse asked.

"You're in the devil's domain, not your own. Who

knows what twists and turns it has up its sleeve that you will need to navigate to get your answer?"

"It wants us to use the chair?" Paranormal Jack Jr. asked.

"Yes, because it knows Clarisse's tendencies and that she would lean toward it."

"So, what do you have for us, Harry?" Clarisse asked with a broken smile.

"The God Helmet; that's what I got. We can use the God Helmet to get the information we need."

They all looked at each other, unsure what Harry was referring to.

"What on Earth is a God Helmet?" Clarisse asked.

"It is scientific research exploring the existence of a 'God gene,' or a genetic component that shows a biologically driven religious tendency and a strongly felt presence of the divine.

"It was inspired by researcher Wilder Persinger, who studied people with epilepsy in the 1950s. During surgeries, Penfield electronically stimulated various brain waves and recorded the patients' sensations, including hearing voices and seeing visions."

Clarisse and Paranormal Jack Jr. shook their heads, unsure what to make of Harry's explanation.

"Do you think you can explain it in layman terms,

Harry, so we can understand it better?" Clarisse asked.

"The God Helmet will open a portal into the demon and spirit world without causing you any harm. That is, you can see the infant spirits in their own dimension. The demon can't penetrate the helmet or play tricks on you. Or, heaven forbid, try to capture your soul."

Silence filled the room as nobody was sure what to make of Harry's idea.

Father O'Connor, who everyone expected would be against the idea, slapped his hand on his thigh. "I think it's worth a try. There's proof of God in all of us, if we're willing to look."

13 THE GOD HELMET

"Something in the brain can produce a religious experience even when it doesn't intend to," Harry explained as he took the God Helmet out of the box and placed it on the table in front of Clarisse. "The presence of God can be developed, regardless of one's religious beliefs, upbringing, or genetics, by simply slipping on this helmet."

Clarisse and Paranormal Jack Jr. shook their heads as Harry proceeded to demonstrate the cased, metallic helmet. It was hard-wired with electrical wires—blue, green, red, and white, twisting in a neat formation, leading to one larger cable protruding from the top.

"You know how I can be regarded as a skeptic, always looking for evidence of the afterlife and the spirit world? Well, the God Helmet solves my inquisitiveness. It merges science and religion into a tool dedicated to investigating what role the brain plays in religious and mystical experiences." Harry stood there, waiting for applause, but all he got was curious looks and bewilderment.

"Do you mind explaining how we're going to use this helmet? I mean, how's this thing going to help us?" Clarisse crossed her arms and raised her eyebrows.

"Well, I've been studying this technology for over a year. I learned the helmet is designed to enhance religious experiences. It stimulates the temporal lobe—that's the part of the brain associated with how we understand God—the amygdala, and hippocampus."

"That's a handful Harry, and I'm glad you understand it," Paranormal Jack Jr. quipped.

Clarisse picked up the helmet and glided her hands over the shiny metal casing to connect with it. "I can feel its energy," she said. She rubbed her hands over it again and closed her eyes. "Do you mind telling me how we are going to use it?" she repeated.

"Without sounding too scientific, the God Helmet utilizes a network of low-intensity magnetic signals, or a field-to-field interaction onto the brain, triggering the left and the right side to communicate."

"What do they communicate?" Paranormal Jack Jr. asked.

"Hmm … A holy presence. The experience of using the

helmet highlights the brain's central role in spirituality normally associated with activities such as prayer, fasting, or meditation."

"That's great Harry, but how does it work? I can see all these wires at the top of the helmet; what do they plug into?" Clarisse was keen on getting answers, but all Harry could do was talk about the technical aspects of the God Helmet.

"Sessions are held in a quiet, acoustic chamber, or totally silent room, with electromagnetic insulation. I plug the wires into my laptop to measure activity, and off we go."

"Where are we going to find an acoustic chamber around here? This is a small town," Paranormal Jack Jr. replied.

Harry nodded. "We'll improvise. I reckon the abortion room is quiet enough to be a silent room. The place is abandoned, so it doesn't get any quieter than Ward C."

"You still haven't explained why you built this helmet." Clarisse smiled as she tapped him on the shoulder. "All those hours away from home, secretly working on this project ... You weren't just working overtime at the office."

"No, I fess up. I had to find time to study and build this helmet, test it, and here you have it, the working prototype. I don't think there's anything like it." Harry took Clarisse's hand and gently rubbed it. "I never forgot what happened with the scarlet chair and how you used it to connect to the spiritual world. Now that's a thing of the past and not necessary. The God Helmet can do that, and you don't need to put yourself in harm's way anymore. And best of all, it's impenetrable—safe from evil interventions."

"What do you mean?" Clarise frowned.

"The external spirit connections you make can't harm you in any way. The God Helmet is designed to exclude all external vibrations and sensory penetration infiltrating the case."

"So, I can contact the spirit world and see their dimension, but they can't mess with me?"

"Yes, it's like a shield."

Clarisse sighed. "You knew I would use the energy of the abortion chair to get into the mind of the evil entity in Ward C."

"After all these years, you think I don't know you?"

Harry took the helmet from Clarisse and placed it on his head. "Now, all you need to do is place the helmet on your head like this and use your natural abilities to connect with the infant spirits, like self-hypnosis."

"That's what the demon wants you to do, Clarisse," Paranormal Jack Jr. interrupted. "To sit on the chair and tap into its energy source so it could—"

"Take my child … the fifth child and complete the curse."

"Yes. That's why Abbey's spirit pointed to you and then the abortion chair. It meant something."

"This devil is slyer than I thought," Clarisse mused. Then she nodded and looked down. "I should've picked up on it, yet it took you to tell me. Huh, maybe I'm losing my touch."

"We're not all perfect. Sometimes we miss things and get distracted," Harry responded. "That's why we're a team; it makes us more effective with our individual strengths."

"So, when do we start?" Paranormal Jack Jr. was keen to try out the new technology.

Harry placed the God Helmet back in the metallic box then closed it. "How about tonight?"

They all looked at each other and nodded.

"Tonight, it is then," Harry said.

"So, how many of these helmets do you have, mate?" Paranormal Jack Jr. asked.

"Hmm … Sounds like you want to give it a try, too. I have two helmets, just in case."

"In case of what?" Clarisse asked.

Harry paused for a moment and thought about his answer. "In case something goes wrong, and we need to pull you back from the spirit world." He smiled and rubbed Clarisse's shoulder. "Every good inventor, or engineer, has a backup plan. Particularly something like this when we're entering an unknown place. We are in the devil's den."

"Yep, it's not a place you want to be stuck in, unable to return. It nearly happened to me in Old Tailem Town with the shaman, so I understand."

"Yeah Clarisse, I remember the shaman had to retrieve you while you were under self-hypnosis, and we don't have anyone like him here."

"It's good you thought ahead, Harry," Paranormal Jack Jr. said.

Harry clasped his hands together and stood up from the table. "Well, let's start getting ready for Willow Court and put the equipment in the Ute."

"Oh, Harry, I want to share something with you that happened in the hospital." Clarisse glanced toward Paranormal Jack Jr., a signal that she needed a moment alone with Harry.

He got the cue and left for the Ute. "I'll get started and meet you outside, Harry."

"What's bothering you, Clarisse?" Harry asked when Paranormal Jack Jr. left the room.

"It's probably nothing, and I don't want you to worry."

Clarisse took Harry's hand and clenched it tightly. "When I was in the hospital, the demon from Hartley visited me. It said I would have complications with my pregnancy, that the obstetrician from Hobart missed my diagnosis."

"Are you sure? Maybe you were dreaming because of the pain killers in your bloodstream." Harry was dismissive.

"I'm sure, Harry, but …"

"But what?"

"I thought about it, and I don't believe it was the demon from Hartley. The timing doesn't make sense—the same demon can't be in two places at the same time—Hartley and New Norfolk?"

"Was it the demon from Willow Court trying to scare you, trick you into thinking it was a demon you're familiar with?"

Clarisse nodded and put on a half-smile.

"Okay, I believe you. And let me tell you something I learned while reading Dr. Monserrat's diary."

"What did you find?"

"This demon has a habit of sneaking up on people and having conversations when you least expect it. Dr. Monserrat documented his conversations with the demon on several occasions."

"Is that so?"

"Yes, and his conclusion was, on each occasion, it used

trickery, lies, and deceit. It became a regular pattern of behavior."

"So, it tried to create a false sense of security?"

"Yes, I guess that's a good way of putting it. It would tell you something bad would happen, and then how it could fix it … at a price, of course." Harry paused for a moment and cleared his throat. "Sometimes, it was telling the truth and other times outright lies. And if you didn't have your wits about, you wouldn't know the difference."

"Let me help you, mate." Paranormal Jack Jr. was excited about the God Helmet and couldn't wait to test it. He took the helmets and loaded them onto the Ute. Harry had a whole bunch of equipment to support the use of the God Helmet.

Harry had developed something quite unique. Though it was experimental and a prototype, there was nothing like it around. What better way than to test it in an authentic setting with someone who could speak to the spirit world?

More importantly, Harry had learned from the events with the scarlet chair and never forgot the pain Clarisse had endured that day. Being able to enter the spirit world with a level of protection meant more people could test their spiritual prowess without being hurt.

Self-hypnosis and the ability to enter the spirit world

were fraught with danger. There was no guarantee what you would encounter on the other side. And, even though it provided glimpses of past events and clues, it was never a foolproof technique.

But there was something else undermining his invention. He knew Clarisse was stubborn, and when she put her mind to something, it was hard to change her point of view. She was six months pregnant, and the demon was after her child, yet she was not one to walk away.

Although they had completed their contractual obligations and had found evidence of spirits at Willow Court, Clarisse did not want to leave the infant spirits. Many other mediums would have given up a long time ago, but not Clarisse. She felt it was her moral duty to save the underlings from their wretched lives. And, like many times before, she wanted to put things right.

She would try to release their souls and show them the way out, to transition to the afterlife and find solace. That was the most effective way to limit the power of a demon and, in some cases, remove its influence altogether.

Clarisse was in for a hell of a battle with the evil of Willow Court. She was carrying a child it wanted so desperately to complete its curse and the Five Points of Calvinism. She was entering its dimension where it had the uttermost authority and influence.

14 THE TULIP

"Clarisse, you need to look for the symbol of the TULIP," Father O'Connor said, standing at the steps of Willow Court Asylum as they arrived with the God Helmets. "I know you're attempting to traverse to the other side."

Harry waved from the pebbled car park, unperturbed by his presence.

"How did you know, Father?" Clarisse asked.

Father O'Connor buttoned up his Cossack as a cold front was passing through New Norfolk. He looked at her as though he wanted to say something else, but only said, "Just look for the TULIP my dear, and follow it." He coughed a little as his throat became sticky. "Take the infant spirits there and show them the way." Father O'Connor then nodded, adjusted his hat, and left Willow

Court, without engaging in any discussion with Harry or Jack Jr.

Clarisse wasn't sure what to think about his impromptu appearance. Father O'Connor had an uncanny way of turning up when you least expected it. But this was the first time he had spoken in riddles.

What about the TULIP? she thought.

Harry pulled up to the steps with Paranormal Jack Jr. carrying the God Helmet cases and other equipment. "What was he doing here?"

"Oh nothing Harry. You know what Father O'Connor's like. He's always hanging around Willow Court Asylum for one reason or another."

Harry nodded, more focused on preparing the God Helmet. "Well, let's make our way to the abortion room and set up." He paused for a moment and looked directly at Clarisse. Then he took her hand.

"Are you sure you want to go through this? Not that I could stop you. You're stubborn, you know."

"Huh, you're always saying that, but maybe I am stubborn." She smiled and took a small bag from Harry's shoulder that was ready to slide off. "Here, let me help you."

Ward C was devoid of any supernatural activity. No

poltergeists, ghosts, or children playing in the background. The usual greeting party of the afterlife was nowhere to be found.

Clarisse thought Father O'Connor's presence was no coincidence. He either had a knack for perfect timing and chance encounters or had worked out their plan. What had he been doing here anyway, giving her advice about the afterlife?

They made haste to the abortion room, walking past the stairs that led to the basement. She looked back to see a glow that lifted from the basement then retreated like a heat signature. There was no sound, vibration, or energy source that she could feel.

As they hastily walked past the rooms in the corridor that once accommodated mental patients, Clarisse saw glimpses of dead people. She shook her head more than once, thinking it was only one room, but that was not the case.

The glimpses of images appeared from every room, standing at the door with the same posture and expressionless body language. They were split-second images that lit up like flash photography then disappeared. It would have been no more than a second on each occasion.

As they walked past the next room, the same thing

happened—a flash of light followed by the monochrome glimpse of a ghost patient. Clarisse shook her head gently and blinked a few times from the after-effects of the monochromatic flashes. They were so bright that she had to readjust her eyes to the dark hallways.

Brilliant light then darkness, one after the other, until they reached the end of the hallway. She was bewildered and taken aback by the display. None of the ghosts said anything or alluded to any potential danger. Furthermore, they were all young women, dressed in nineteenth century attire and hairstyles of that day. It was like a snapshot in time.

Harry looked back and saw Clarisse falling behind, disorientated, and unable to keep up; stopping at every room, glancing inside, and then rubbing her eyes before she moved on to the next room. Harry and Paranormal Jack Jr. saw nothing, but dead spirits could speak to Clarisse and manifest themselves to her. It came with her spirit hunter tag—evil spoke to her.

This would have worried him, but Harry had become accustomed to her unique qualities in Hartley and Old Tailem Town. He understood she was tapping into energy sources in every room.

He tugged on her arm then gripped her hand. "We need to get to the abortion room, Clarisse," he said, encouraging her to move on. Sometimes she needed to be brought back to reality, and then she would snap out of it.

Clarisse turned to Harry and squinted. "They're everywhere, you know—all the patients, the sadness, and the misery of this place."

Harry nodded in understanding. He wasn't going to fight it. Clarisse was warming up, and her senses were in a heightened state, ready for the God Helmet and to enter the spirit world of the infant spirits. In a way, she was preparing herself for self-hypnosis.

Inside the abortion room, Harry knew time was of the essence. They needed to set up the equipment quickly and prepare the God Helmet for Clarisse. Harry was sure the evil entity was monitoring their activities. The spare one was on standby for Paranormal Jack Jr.

The room had an eerie sense of hate. It was a hurtful place, filled with death and misery. Nothing good emanated from this theatre of horrors.

Clarisse referred to the room as being dead with the energy of despair absorbed into the objects, such as the abortion chair and the utensils on the table. The negative energy source had to take hold of something to stay alive and couldn't float around endlessly. This was what made the room morbid in every way.

"Are you ready, Clarisse?" Harry asked.

Clarisse sat in a metallic chair that blended into the misery of the room. She nodded in acknowledgment.

Harry powered up his laptop, connected the primary cable to the tip of the God Helmet, and then placed it on Clarisse's head. He tightened the strap underneath her chin and winked at her.

"Don't self-hypnotize until I set up Jack's helmet, okay?"

Paranormal Jack Jr. decided to place the God Helmet on his own head. He rubbed his thumb along his cheek, unperturbed by what to expect and symptomatic of his personality—no fear, a do now and think later mentality.

"Okay, we're set." Harry powered up the instruments, and a sequence of flashing lights circled the God Helmet.

"I feel the energy," Clarisse said. She looked toward Harry and Paranormal Jack Jr., signaling she was ready for self-hypnosis.

Her face twitched a few times, and she creased her lips as though she was chewing on something. She closed her eyes, although you could see her pupils flicking underneath her eyelids. The God Helmet was manipulating her temporal lobe while she entered self-hypnosis and transitioned to the spirit world. The pulsating lights on the God Helmet pulsated at an alarming speed—in microseconds.

As for Paranormal Jack Jr., on standby, his God Helmet was not powered up. Should Clarisse encounter any anomalies, he would need to self-hypnotize and retrieve her.

Clarisse would describe his level of expertise in self-hypnosis as emerging and with potential. He was in the learning stage that they all had to endure. She'd had a good teacher in the shaman at Old Tailem Town. She had learned from trial and error; sometimes putting herself at unnecessary risk.

Clarisse arrived in the spirit world—a dark cavern of nothingness with only a speckle of light leading to a partially opened door ten feet away. There was an eerie silence, as though sound was filtered. Any mortal way of deciphering your environment, like touch, feel, smell, and taste, didn't work here. It was a black blanket, smothering any signs of life

She walked toward the door instinctively. That was what her heightened senses were asking her to do. Something awaited on the other side. Still, she remembered the words of Father O'Connor—*look for the TULIP.*

When she arrived at the door, it opened to a haze; a gentle nightlight, sufficient to look around only. She was in a cavern of death, a transient world that spirits endlessly navigated their way into and out of regularly but usually going nowhere, caught in a never-ending spiral of nothingness. It was like walking in circles in a dark forest at night without a guide to recognize nature's markers. Essentially, in this place you were lost with no timestamp or sense of being. That was what it was like for the infant spirits. However, they wouldn't have known any better. Too young to understand the difference between their world and our own dimension. They probably didn't even know they were dead.

Clarisse walked farther into the room. The images of four children awaited her—two boys and two girls. They were the same children whom she had encountered in Ward C.

The older girl was holding a Teddy bear and the hand of the younger boy. A child who was the oldest of the two boys fiddled with marbles as he flicked them in the air and caught them before they fell to the ground. They stood there, emotionless, stoic faces, and innocent. How many times over the past hundred and fifty years had they performed this same routine?

The oldest child spoke to her, but not verbally, through the God Helmet. A connection was being made by way of thought.

"*Can you take us home?*" the girl asked, clutching her bear then rubbing it along her face. She raised her arm and pointed to her right.

Another door with light emanating softly partially opened. But this door was different—a red tulip lay on the ground. It was the only source of color in this place of dark grey shades.

Something pulled Clarisse to the tulip as she recalled Father O'Connor's words. It was the way out. Clarisse had to direct them to the tulip.

"*Go to the tulip, all of you together,*" Clarisse communicated with the infant spirits through the God Helmet.

The oldest girl nodded then turned to the other children. They all took hold of each other's hands, and together they walked in a straight line toward the door with the red tulip. It was time to transition to the afterlife and leave their transient nonexistence.

The tulip had always been there, showing up from time to time. Still, they were not inquisitive enough to understand what it meant—that it was a signpost to the afterlife.

Instead, the evil entity had flooded their thoughts with games and playfulness. It had let them out to play in a big room with no one to boss them around. There had been no rules.

As children, we were limited to free expression from the time we were born. *Don't do this. Don't do that. You must do it this way and not that way.* Those constraints didn't exist in the playground of Ward C. They were dead, lost, and unaware. But, like any child, they embraced the freedom of expression not bound by any parental conditioning. Only an intelligent demon could hold them together with such a carrot dangling in front of them.

But the demon had underestimated the call of a mother. A playground with no rules was no replacement for the hugs and love a mother could provide a child.

As the infants walked toward the door with the red tulip, a group of mothers appeared on the other side, of which three stood out in front, calling them over by waving, encouraging them to take the final step. It reminded Clarisse of what her mother would do—waiting at the classroom doorstep every day to pick her up, waving, then caressing her with a big hug. The thought sent a chill right through her. Nothing could replace a mother's love for a child.

Then Abbey's ghost appeared behind the children. She was unsure of what to do and looked confused. And, unlike her presence in the abortion room, this time she was fully visible, precisely as she would have been before she had died.

She took hold of her son's hand and resisted the attempt to follow the other children. Still caught under the spell of the demon and the pact she had made, the devil controlled her every move.

"*Go to the door with the tulip. Follow the other children,*" Clarisse pleaded with her thoughts, encouraging Abbey to make a move while she had the opportunity, to break away from the demon's influence.

"You need to go in now!" Harry said. "Jack, you need to retrieve Clarisse and pull her back. Something is fighting her."

"How do you know?" Paranormal Jack Jr. asked.

"Can't you see her face? Her cheeks are vibrating, and her eyelids are moving frantically."

From a distance, Clarisse's whole body was shivering, and the pulsating lights around the God Helmet flashed faster than before. The God Helmet was heating up with electric impulses.

Paranormal Jack Jr. tightened the helmet into position then strapped it around his chin. He closed his eyes as Harry switched on the electromagnetic pulses from his laptop. His eyelids flickered, and his lips tensed up, just like Clarisse's had. He was grinding his teeth while his body remained still. Then Paranormal Jack Jr. was transposed to the same dimension as Clarisse.

On the other side, Clarisse was being attacked by the demon entity, desperate to stop its flock of children from reaching the exit gates and transitioning to the afterlife. It was a face of two halves; one side orange color while the other was dark grey, as though a shadow had been cast over it. It had the facial contours of a human—a chiseled, edged chin, a western-style nose, and flawless skin. Its contoured eyes were thick with eyeliner but otherwise almond-shaped, with black pupils that penetrated right through you.

Taking more of the human form than the devilish attributes in appearance, it wore a headpiece of shining silver with protruding circular designs, like a stag with antlers, such was the intricate design. It was a demon unlike any she had encountered before.

The demon gripped her right ankle with its long hands and elegant fingers, like a piano player but with protruding bear-like nails. It pricked and dug into her skin as she tried desperately to kick it away, but each time, its grip became tighter.

She glanced at the demon's face, but she could not communicate with it, as it wasn't allowing her to.

Unlike other demon encounters, this evil entity did not resemble a frightening beast. It was more refined and elegant. Was it a prince from hell?

It pulled Clarisse toward it while she fell on her back, desperately trying to resist its wrath. Nevertheless, the demon kept tugging her.

There were no obstacles in the room to cling to. Clarisse couldn't even feel herself sliding. It was like treading water in a pool without the splashes of water and unable to touch the bottom.

Clarisse could see the infant spirits from the corner of her eye, in reach of the tulip and the exit door to the afterlife. To her surprise, she found Abbey leading the way now, taking charge, like any mother would. Walking all four children to the exit, they were just about there and knocking on freedom's door. Their souls would traverse to the afterlife and find peace, released from the clutches of the devil and its infinite control. They would embrace their mothers firmly with hugs and kisses.

While being sucked toward the devil, she had a chance to smile. The demon would not get the fifth child and complete its curse. The Five Points of Calvinism would remain under the influence of the Catholic church.

Right then, Paranormal Jack Jr. appeared next to Clarisse and reached out for her, clasping her hand firmly.

It became a tug of war between them and the devil.

While there was no sound in this dimension, and he could not speak directly with her, he quickly learned to communicate through his thoughts.

"*Close your eyes and disconnect from the hypnosis,*" he thought, hoping Clarisse would hear him. He kept repeating the same thought. "*Disconnect. Disconnect now!*"

You couldn't scream in this world of spirits, as it was an empty space with no air, wind, sun, or rain. Nothing.

While Paranormal Jack Jr. persisted with his thoughts, he also had a realization. *Is this where death takes us? Do we all end up here?* He looked around and caught a glimpse of the infant spirits walking through a door that expelled a soft neon light. They held their mothers tightly, embraced, and then one by one, they disappeared with a twinkle of a star.

Was that the undoing of the demon?

Paranormal Jack Jr. suddenly felt the pull of the demon wither away until he was no longer required to tug her. Clarisse's child held no value for the devil anymore, as it couldn't complete its curse. It needed five newborn children and now it had none.

Clarisse returned to the abortion room, shaken but unharmed. Next to her was Paranormal Jack Jr., clasping his hands together in a fist. Staring at her was Harry as he gently slapped her on the cheek many times to ensure that she was back in the current dimension.

Paranormal Jack Jr. took off the God Helmet and placed it beside him. Then he slid his hands over his face and looked down while taking a deep breath.

"We did it, we did it," Clarisse repeated as she removed her God Helmet then embraced Harry tightly. A tear rolled down the side of her face, and she sighed.

"They're free?" Harry whispered.

"Yes. And Abbey, too."

Clarisse raised her head slightly from Harry's embrace and looked toward the door of the abortion room. Father O'Connor was standing there silently and holding his hands together over his abdomen, a typical pose for a priest. But, why did Father O'Connor have a stethoscope around his neck with the insignia GLM (George Lawrence Monserrat)?

Father O'Connor smiled and made the sign of the cross. Then he nodded to her. It was as though a dark veil had been lifted from his soul as he left the room.

THE END

ABOUT THE AUTHOR

Janice is an Australian author who lives with her family in Melbourne. Her recent publication, *Haunting in Old Tailem*, reached number one on the Amazon kindle ranking for Occult, Supernatural, and Ghosts and Haunted Houses categories, for hot new releases and bestsellers.

Janice is a finalist in the Readers' Favorite 2020 International Book Awards in fiction-supernatural and was awarded the distinguished favorite prize for paranormal horror at the New York City Big Book Awards 2020. She recently received a silver medal at the 2021 IPPY Book Awards for Australia/New Zealand/Pacific Rim—Best Regional Fiction.

Janice is well-versed in her cultural superstitions and how they influence daily life and customs. She has developed a passion and style for writing ghost and supernatural novels for new adult readers.

Her books contain heart-thumping, bone-chilling, thought-provoking ghosts and paranormal experiences that deliver a new twist to every tale.

https://www.janicetremayne.com

HAUNTING CLARISSE SUPERNATURAL HORROR SERIES

She never signed up to be a spirit fighter. Hunting down demons? But evil spoke to Clarisse and changed her life forever.

Enjoy over 800 pages of intense, nail-biting, and spine-tingling demonic encounters in real Australian ghost towns.

Clarisse never imagined her first encounter with demons would be in her own home. A scarlet chair with a two-hundred-year-old curse, bound by superstition. Hell-bent on destroying relationships, this evil presence wants her out of the way.

She meets her soul mate and joins him in visiting remote ghost towns. But supernatural battles lay waiting as local demons summon her. Can she convince her skeptical partner that it takes more than intuition to rid these towns of entrenched evil?

Can Clarisse withstand the sharp-talking demons that latch on to her with sinister motives? Will she cleanse the ghost towns from their curse?

These evil encounters become an affliction of the mind; a risk to herself and her partner that could result in death.

https://www.amazon.com/dp/B08HGPL2G5

Made in United States
North Haven, CT
09 September 2024

57164166R00146